Alas Poor Father!

JOAN FLEMING

Alas Poor Father!

G. P. Putnam's Sons, New York

FIRST AMERICAN EDITION 1973

Copyright © 1972 by Joan Fleming

SBN: 399-11089-5

Library of Congress Catalog
Card Number: 72-90808

Third Impression

Printed in the United States of America

1

"She's dead," James said, giving her a slight push with his foot.

"Don't kick her!" Joshua exclaimed crossly.

"I wasn't kicking her," James returned steadily.

Joshua, always overemotional, flung himself upon the grass and wept bitterly and somewhat noisily. These outbursts were always deathly embarrassing to his older brother, but this time James, too, was upset, perhaps even more so than Joshua; noisy grief is more bearable than silent grief. With Joshua's face in the grass, James knelt down and gently turned over the little stiff body with the hard round yellow eye, like the bead eye of a child's stuffed toy, and tears of anguish filled his eyes as he saw the ugly purple patch of dried blood staining the gentle gray head feathers. Characteristically he dashed to the tumbled-down garden shed and snatched up a spade; behind their shabby little pigeon loft he started energetically to dig while his brother's cries increased in force as his feelings started to recover from the shock; he had dug a hole nearly two feet deep by the time the wailing ceased altogether. His brother lay still, face downward on the grass, listening acutely.

"There!" James came out from behind the loft. "Should we wrap her in a winding sheet?"

Joshua sat up. "Winding sheet? There's one of Father's old socks in the rag bag behind the scullery door . . . that might do. I'll go and get it. . . ."

It was a hateful job pushing the gray feathered body into the sock; they started tail first then had to turn it to slide it in the direction the feathers lay; that way it was easy, head first and breast upward, but Joshua had a long, careful look at the wound. "So she was shot!" He started whimpering. "I'll kill them!"

"Kill who?"

"Whoever did it."

"But who could it have been?" James asked. He thought he knew who it could have been: the only person nearby who owned a rook rifle, the son of the nearest farmer.

Holding the loaded sock between them, they stared at one another.

"I said . . . *I'll kill him!*"

Carrying their burden between them, they moved behind the pigeon loft and gently laid their beloved in the hole already prepared. Quickly, quickly so that it was no longer in their sight, they covered up the navy blue woolen-clad bundle, James using the spade, and Joshua, still whimpering, sniffing and stopping to wipe his nose on the back of his hand, clawing at the gummy clay soil with his fingers.

When the disturbed ground was smoothed over, James straightened up and stood at attention, crossing himself and saying soberly: "RIP." Joshua, slightly peeved that he had not thought of it himself, pretended to have a little more work on the grave to complete. Then he, too, stood up, crossed himself and said: "Ditto!"

They then opened the trapdoor and picked out of the old bird bay the mourning widower.

"Do you think he knows?"

"Of course he does, he was waiting for her to come home. How shall we dare ever again to leave him out on the roof?" James held the bird's beak to his warm cheek, comforting.

"We must give him an extra-good supper." Joshua energetically opened the cupboard at the bottom of the loft and took out a handful of corn, which he sprinkled on the floor of the bay. Mr. O'Duff had told him, over and over again, not to be sloppy about feeding and leave the corn sprinkled about for constant snacks, but anxiety overlaid the rules, and he added to the irregularity by tearing up a handful of fresh young dandelion leaves and thrusting them inside.

"But Father is away!" James remembered. "He's in town today!"

Joshua scowled horribly, trying to come to terms with the unwelcome news that his father was not the murderer

6

of their lovely hen pigeon. He didn't answer, but took the widower from his brother and replaced him in the empty nesting box with the utmost care.

Picking up the school satchel, he hooked it over his arm and they both wandered disconsolately up the little garden path, brushing aside the clean washing left by Mrs. Flower for them to bring in after tea, James' arm thrown across his brother's shoulder.

"Oh . . . look!" Joshua screamed, a cry of despair. The Rolls-Royce parked in the drive outside the lodge was so big that a yard or so of the yellow hood could easily be seen from the back garden.

"Let's hide!" But it was too late, a screech comparable to that of a hysterical peacock or mother peahen, heralded the appearance of their pet aversion, Mrs. Desirée Furnish, JP.

Not that it was a surprise; she had this habit of turning up at any time of the day or, for that matter, night. She came, as always, bearing gifts, succor, which she was convinced was always required, and suggestions for ameliorating the awful lot of a womanless man with a family of two schoolboys, living in a rented, poky gatehouse.

"There you are, dears!" she screeched, emerging from the french windows of the living room, her arms widely spread not hopefully but in a general gesture of largess. "Where's Daddy?"

James, acutely conscious of the sudden gap beside him, walked steadily forward. "In London. . . . Yes, he had a telephone call late last night," he continued with some satisfaction. "He went on the eight fifteen."

"And what time is he coming back?"

James shrugged his shoulders, bitterly resenting her. "No idea. . . ."

Ignoring his manner completely, she said she might meet the train, and James sullenly replied that as his father had taken himself to the station in his own car, why bother?

"Why bother? Because I do bother about you, about you all, James. For instance, what about your tea?"

"We don't have it till Father comes home from your place at five thirty."

"What about tonight, since you don't know when he'll be home?"

"Oh, I expect Mrs. Flower will have left something. . . ." James brushed past her on his way into the living room that Mrs. Flower called the lounge, to start his homework.

"Well, I shall get myself a cup of tea, even if you boys don't want any," Mrs. Furnish said in a brave try at being a welcome visitor.

Joshua lay in the large armchair usually occupied by their father, in front of the television, which he had turned on. He looked inordinately small, his bony, dirty knees stuck up and outward, watching the television through the V his limbs formed. The picture the screen was showing was almost completely dark, but sounds of gasping and groans were coming from it.

"He's lost in a London sewer," Joshua exclaimed, holding his nose demonstratively. "Coo, the smell!"

James settled down to his homework, which he seemed prepared to do in spite of the noise, and presently, Mrs. Furnish came in with a tray of tea things. Neither of the boys took any notice, but after she had poured out a cup for herself and started sipping she said, brow knotted: "You mean you have *high* tea?"

"Coo . . . look at that," Joshua groaned, hugging himself in anguish. A man lay on the floor, apparently bleeding profusely; then with darkened looks Joshua scowled. "Have you got a gun, Mrs. Furnish?" He made her name sound like an insult.

"Have I got a gun!" A tinkle of silvery laughter. "My dear boy, I've a whole lot of guns. They were my husband's and they're kept in the gun room in glass cases"—she waved an arm vaguely—"all round the walls, you know." And she added, "The cases are kept locked, of course."

"Well, that's funny," Joshua said lugubriously, "because our racing hen pigeon was shot dead whilst we were at school. We left her on the roof of the loft; we've trained her to go back inside through the trap after a little fly around, she's reliable, but someone shot her."

"Not I, dear boy. Can you imagine it? Taking out one of the guns I never touch and don't even know how to load;

8

driving eight miles to shoot one of your pets; going home and putting the gun away. . . ." She spoke soberly, and James looked up with grudging admiration; she was not talking down to Joshua, but on a level, as though he were an adult, which was perhaps more than he deserved.

"It must have been one of the village boys with a semitoy gun," she suggested reassuringly, "trigger-happy. How very mean!"

"But school's started again," James pointed out. "We come back on the bus, and all the bigger boys come back on the same bus."

"Well, it was a very mean thing to do. You'll have to start doing some sleuthing, won't you? Listen, dears, I'll buy you another. . . ."

They were staggered, but Joshua unwound himself out of the big chair and turned off the television. He managed not to say, "Now you're talking." He sat down on a hard chair, facing her with knees apart, giving his whole attention to her; in this mood Joshua could be irresistible. Both the boys were good-looking; neither of their faces had started that unruly adolescent growth of the features that has to be endured by the adolescent male for a varying number of years and is hard to bear.

The telephone rang in the hall, and as neither of the boys seemed to be going to answer it, Mrs. Furnish did so.

"Yes," they heard her say, "this is Brigadier Patricott's house. Who is speaking, please? The Foreign Office? Would you like me to give him a message? Sir Francis Ansdell. You'll ring again. Yes. . . ."

She returned to her tea drinking and the boys went on where the conversation had been left off. "But those pigeons are special, very special *racing* pigeons . . . sometimes they cost hundreds of pounds. Mr. O'Duff gave us these two last October. They were late-hatched, and we've been feeding them and looking after them all winter, and they were mated, and she laid two eggs. And later on she was going to win races!"

As Joshua's voice rose hysterically almost to a wail, James took over: "Mr. O'Duff is training us, you see, so that we can be pigeon fanciers and have racing pigeons which win races, like he does. He said if we could keep the pigeons in good health and condition until the mating season, that was a good start. The food is very expensive, you see, cod-liver oil and vitamins and special kinds of corn . . . and Josh and I have had to earn the money to keep them, at weekends, doing odd jobs, you know . . . mowing lawns and weeding and things—"

In the unfortunate squashing way she had, which was one of the things they so much resented, she said that their father had told her all about it, puncturing their enthusiasm and sending them right back into themselves. They shut up like clams.

Realizing she had put herself in the wrong, she tried redress by saying that she quite understood how difficult their lives had been, moving about the Middle East for years with no fixed abode and, above all, no mother. She understood quite well how the brigadier had come to retire so early from the army, and they should realize what a sacrifice their father had made for their well-being. She, personally, admired him, their father, very much indeed. As an Arabist of distinction he could have had a very fine job if he had been willing to continue his nomadic life, but he had deliberately thrown it all up for his boys and settled down "at the back o' beyond, helping out an old widow with her greenhouses." This last was said with intent to please.

Sulkily they regarded her with a "well, so what?" expression on their faces. They had been talking about pigeons, hadn't they?

James said argumentatively that their father had always called England "home" and had always wanted to retire and live here forever: "He's hardly ever lived here since he was eighteen. . . ."

But what he was saying was rendered entirely incoherent because Joshua was speaking at the same time and Joshua was also saying argumentatively that pigeons had to be bred and not just bought off the cuff, like that, Mr. O'Duff said so. There was no fun racing a pigeon that wasn't *your* pigeon. But still, he said it only half-convinced because, of course, offers are not to be disregarded, however unrealistic they might be. They subsided into silence again.

Mrs. Furnish tidied up her tea tray and seemed to be preparing to leave.

"There are four kippers in the fridge. Is that going to be your evening meal?"

"Why not?" James said challengingly. "We love kippers. Mrs. Flower must have bought them from the fish van which comes round."

"You can't maintain growing boys on kipper teas," she said in the rich round voice she used on committees.

"Kippers are herrings," James argued tenaciously, "and I learned in biology kippers are herrings and herrings contain more nourishment than any other fish."

She stood now, tray in hand, and looked at them, sighing a loud artificial sigh. As the door shut behind her, Joshua said, "Silly interfering bitch!" He turned on the television. "Belt up!" he shouted above the noise.

But she heard, and it was then she left the lodge to wander up the drive, in search perhaps of this O'Duff who seemed to have so much influence upon these two young boys.

2

Short, stout males are usually associated with cheerful, round faces and lighthearted manner; they often have a sprightly, light-footed tread and hair going thin on top . . . unless they don't. Basil Patricott, known as Buzz by his friends, was one of the exceptions, though he wore the habitual look of anxiety which sits unaccountably upon some brigadiers. In this particular brigadier's case there was much to account for the worried expression. Firstly, and most of all, he had not, and never would, get over the death of his young wife from cancer at the age of thirty.

11

Secondly, he could not decide, with any degree of certainty, how best to bring up his two boys. Thirdly, the thought of having any other woman as a wife, to have and to hold until death, etc., was entirely nauseating. Fourthly, a number of women had pointed out to him how important it was for the boys to have a "mother," and some, indeed, had suggested themselves as likely candidates for this job, but this only increased the brigadier's revulsion to the idea. Fifthly, he agreed with them in principle, which made things much worse, but the constant endeavor to succeed in bringing the boys successfully to an age when they might be considered no longer to need his care, was undermined by a strong awareness of his own shortcomings.

It was not actually that he had failed in his career; he had not. He could speak and read Arabic with a fluency seldom found in an Englishman and had proved himself invaluable to the army. Furthermore, he had on several occasions since his retirement been of assistance to the Foreign Office in matters connected with such esoteric business as new constitutions for "emerging countries" and bargaining with oil sheikhs.

Nobody quite knew what these occasional excursions were, since everything connected with the Foreign Office is so hush-hush as to be unmentionable. Indeed, the brigadier himself would wonder occasionally of what whole his contributions constituted a part. One single fact only gave him no cause for anxiety, and that was that these assignations had nothing whatever to do with spying. He made quite sure of that before starting. "It's not that I'm against spying in principle," he had explained to the FO, "but I'm responsible for these two youngsters of mine." They had understood perfectly.

As he stepped down from the London train at six fifty, carrying his important black dispatch case with a padlock and with the royal insignia on it under his arm (alas, it contained only the *Evening Standard,* a clean pair of socks and half a meat pie he could not manage to eat at lunchtime), he felt that the regret with which he was going to turn down the next job offered him by Frank Ansdell should be disregarded in relation to the larger sacrifice he had reluctantly decided to make for his little family. *Only good can come of it,* his mother used to say, as he did something she wished when he very much wanted to do something else.

As he handed in his ticket, his expression of anxiety by no means lifted, because he was wondering now whether the pickup would start—it had been making some queer noises on the way to the station early this morning.

He started back with a grunt of distress at the great shadow the Rolls-Royce made across the window of the ticket hall, and he cowered down behind a huge man carrying two suitcases. But it was in vain that he tried to escape what awaited him; she was standing right in the doorway of the ticket hall.

"There you are, Buzz!" She gave such a loud cry that several people looked around to see who was being greeted with such enthusiasm.

He at once remonstrated that, lovely though it was of her to meet him, he couldn't possibly avail himself of her offer to take him home, because the pickup was in the station approach, left there this morning.

But she took his arm, and though she was but slightly taller than he, she gave the impression of bending over him persuasively; only a complete cad could have shaken her off in full view of the whole county coming home for the weekend.

"Don't worry, darling," she said as she started up the engine of her car, "we're only going to the Woolstapler's Arms. I must, I simply must talk to you!"

And later, in a warm corner of the bar, away from the crowd, she persuaded him to have dinner there with her as she reached for the large menu, as big as a notice board, that was being handed round.

"Don't worry," she insisted, "the boys don't know when you're coming home, on this or the later train . . . if you don't turn up in twenty minutes or so they will have two kippers each, since Mrs. Flower left four and three into four is an awkward kind of sharing. . . ."

He thought about the half meat pie in his case; it would be nice not to have to eat it while the boys shared the fourth kipper.

He said: "Mrs. Flower does her best; she's a poor widder woman, as you call yourself so erroneously. She really is poor. . . ."

His hostess didn't want to talk about Mrs. Flower; she interrupted him impatiently, but he doggedly insisted on finishing his sentence.

". . . kippers are a feast to her; she has them on a Friday evening, and now her daughter is married and away and her son in London, she has two, two kippers to herself, she told me."

Mrs. Furnish clicked her tongue impatiently.

The Woolstapler's Arms put on an excellent dinner, and after the gins in the bar they had a bottle of Meursault . . . and another.

"You're trying to get me drunk," the brigadier said soberly.

"I know you well enough to know I'll never succeed in that; I'm trying to get myself drunk, if anything, because I have something important to talk to you about, Buzz darling. You'll have to drive me home and bring the car back and leave it at the station, so you can drive yourself home in that awful tin can you're so careful of."

But he was quite enjoying himself; he only half listened to what she was saying because he had heard most of it before. He enjoyed the excellent *pâté maison*, the sirloin steak with Parmesan cheese, and the ice cream with tiny macaroons floating in Cointreau. It is not easy to be constructively argumentative when your stomach is having a splendid treat; after the coffee and brandies he drove her in her Rolls the ten miles to her large red-brick house built in 1901, with its overhanging black and white "Elizabethan" gables.

He didn't like her; nothing she did could possibly make him like her. Basically she was the sort of woman he detested, large, good-looking, madly sure of herself, managing, loud . . . oh, everything he hated. It didn't make any difference that she was kind and generous and employed him in doing what all his life he had done as a hobby and what he enjoyed doing very much. Strangely

14

enough, none of this made him like her any better.

For a year and a half now he had had her warm excellent greenhouse to himself. He had grown a fine crop of tomatoes, the proceeds from the sale of which had gone into improvements to the heating, and he had been free to try out poinsettia and azalea and cyclamen, which had sold easily at Christmas. He felt he was as happy in his work as anyone could be, and thus he had been able to control his basic dislike up to now. If he felt anything other than a warm felicity after the meal it was confidence that he had the situation under control: the danger time, in fact.

Sunk deep in a pink chair in an essentially pink drawing room in front of a huge electric fire throwing out sunlike rays of heat, he was happily relaxed, while she sat in a pink damask-covered knowle settee.

She told him that she had been along to the lodge this afternoon to see him and found the boys back from school and upset about the death of one of their pigeons.

"They seem to think I might have shot it." She laughed merrily. "I know they don't like me but . . . I thought that was going a bit far!"

"Oh, dear! Take no notice, I'm sorry."

"And, Buzz," she went on in a confidential voice, "this friend or so-called benefactor of the boys, this man O'Duff up at the big house. Don't you think he's a bit of a strange character?"

"As Irish as they come . . ." he replied sleepily. "He's kindness itself to the boys . . . he's fixed them up with a hobby I couldn't have thought up in a hundred years. . . ." He chuckled.

"Yes, but . . . that big house and he lives in the scullery quarters . . . I don't understand him. I must admit I felt it my duty to explore a bit. I went up there this afternoon after the boys' tea. . . ."

He felt irritated but less so than if he had not dined regally. He looked at her reproachfully. "Are you implying anything, my dear?"

She reddened and looked flustered.

"Because please don't. I've met O'Duff, of course, and

15

though eccentric, I found him a perfectly decent man, his mind full of nothing but his hobby; rather a bore about it if anything. . . ."

She ran a nervous finger over her lips, obviously wondering how best to continue.

"Don't let's spoil our evening out!" he said irritably.

She looked put out for a moment; then leaving her seat on the high-backed sofa, she knelt beside his chair and one hand came forward and rested on his knee. "Buzz, you'll have to face reality some time, you know. It is bad for those boys to be as much together as they are without any friends. . . ."

"They've had to be together and look to one another for companionship in the life we've led; schools all over the Middle East; I reckon they've been to five different schools, they haven't had time to make friends with other kids. . . ."

"But they have now you're out of the army and becoming a horticulturist."

"Well, they're going to a state school I'm quite pleased with. . . ."

"Oh, Buzz! You are an exasperating darling! If ever two boys ought to be at a boarding school, it's those two."

"Don't make me laugh," the brigadier muttered soberly. "A thousand a year before we even start counting: clothes, pocket money, tuck, extras, railway fare. No, no! Not for us. Give us time, they'll make friends."

"They won't, they are absolutely engrossed in their own pursuits and that idiot up at the house, O'Duff. What sort of companion is he for their leisure hours?"

And so it went on, leading up gradually, as he realized too late, to the inevitable climax. Too late, but he stretched out his feet toward the heat pouring at him from the electric fire and let the criticism flow over him.

She went on that she could pay their school fees, why not? In this day and age why be proud? She had far too much money. You didn't often find people around who admitted to having too much money, but he could ask her accountants (as if he would!). They were begging her to make some large capital expenditure to reduce her really

16

shockingly high income tax. This would be a splendid opportunity; famous schools nowadays were only too ready to receive a capital sum in lieu of termly payment.

Still relaxed, he allowed her to continue, to go on and on about his duty to the boys and how absolutely essential it was for their future good that they should go to a boarding school, a good one, mind. . . .

And then there was a very long silence, a silence which could be construed as a period of thinking the proposition over.

And then, somehow or other, he was in her arms, and he was being rocked as though he were a baby. He was feeling horror and anger but, most strangely of all, he was feeling pity, a desperate sadness. Very gently he wriggled out of her clutches; he practically choked as he struggled with her name, the name she had often begged him to use: Desirée.

He rose to the occasion valiantly, gently pointing out that he could accept her patronage up to the point of receiving a weekly wage from her as a worker in the hothouse, but that he could not accept anything further and he could not explain why, but that was that.

"If we were married, everything would be all right," she moaned, her face hidden from him in her hands.

"Thank you, thank you," he was horrified to hear himself saying politely. "It's wonderful of you to offer but it's—it's completely impossible."

"You hate me, Buzz, I've felt it in my bones. . . ."

"No, no, no!" He patted her gently on the nearest arm. "Nonsense!"

"Think it over, my darling man. Don't be hasty, think it over and you will come round to it. I need a man here in this house; it's far too big for me. If you think it over long enough, you'll come round to it because it is the answer to all your problems. . . ."

He wished unbearably that he had the old pickup standing outside instead of the great limousine waiting for him to drive to his pad. If the pickup were outside, he could walk out and leave her *now*. But to walk out and step into her car and drive back home in haste somehow was not possible. With his hands pressed between his knees he sat on the edge of the sofa and suffered. Finally, driven to some initiative, he suggested they go into the kitchen and make coffee "because I'm not in a fit condition to get myself safely home in your car!"

Nothing could have been less cozy and *intime* than the huge, empty, spotless kitchen. He stood awkwardly beside the table, not knowing where anything was kept; she switched on an electric percolator and in silence laid out the cups, found the sugar and cream, and all the time avoided looking at him.

Finally she said: "The boys think you'll be going away on one of your missions to the Middle East. Somebody telephoned from the Foreign Office to speak to you whilst I was there this afternoon. I can't remember his name."

"Frank Ansdell?"

She nodded.

"Yes, he wouldn't take no for an answer this morning, when I saw him at the FO. Sent me off to 'think it over.' I've been asked to 'think over' something very important twice today, this morning at the FO and now this evening with you. . . . Why can't people take it that you're quite certain the first time you say no and don't need time for thinking it over?"

It was as though he were talking to himself; he muttered moodily: "It's easier to say no the first time, that's why. People . . . they think you'll have second thoughts, or they think you'll listen to reason, or they think they'll be able to brainwash you into thinking their way. Well, when I say no, I mean no, and that's not because I'm a strong man, I know I'm not, I'm probably a weak one, so I have to be pigheaded. If you come to think of it, the weaker the chap, the more stubborn and difficult it is to make him change his mind." And he added for civility, as though just remembering her presence: "Desirée."

She said: "It's because of the boys you can't accept this proposition, isn't it?"

And when he didn't answer, she went on slyly, goading him: "You could always have your mother down here to look after them whilst you are away."

18

He burst out angrily: "Of course I couldn't!"

She poured out the coffee, and sitting on one herself, she indicated the stool beside the table.

"My mother has a tiny two-roomed flat on a long lease, between Westminster Abbey and the Army and Navy Stores, and she is perfectly contented; that's one problem I don't have. She took the boys to Bognor in the summer for three weeks, which was a success; I would not, nor would I want to, ask anything else of her. I'm fond of her, she's one of those mothers who never expect anything much of their sons."

Desirée sniffed but quickly turned it into a simple nose blowing.

As he stirred his coffee, the brigadier turned over in his mind the mess he was now in; he did not see how he could continue to work in her greenhouse. One good thing, as he put it, he had found in his rich employer was that she was allergic to tomato plants; thus for two-thirds of last year he was left alone with his crop. She had haunted him when the tomatoes were over before Christmas during the cyclamen season, but now she was discovering an allergy to geranium cuttings and the pelargoniums, so he was alone once more, happy in his work.

He was not a mean-minded man, he told himself; he was ready to give credit where credit was due. He would readily admit that his dislike of Desirée could well be a personal idiosyncrasy, but admission of this could not cure it. The financial easement that would come of marriage with the "old bean" would never outweigh the satisfaction of not being thus enslaved. Some men would think him a damn fool . . . however, there it was!

"I must be going, my dear. . . ."

There ensued a scene over which, for decency's sake, a veil must be drawn.

3

It was not so very late when he arrived home; he felt distinctly surprised that the hall clock had not reached midnight. The coffee had been a mistake, he realized as he undressed; he had had several cups without cream, and he felt as wide awake as he felt wretched. He hopefully turned out the light and lay on his back in the dark. Life for him, he reflected, was difficult, unwieldy, intractable; he compared himself to a boy of seven endeavoring to advance across a river in a punt but finding the punt pole refractory, in fact impossible to handle. He did not find the ordinary business of living easy.

Much as he enjoyed working in the greenhouse he would be forced to give it up; he wanted never to see his benefactress again. A lot of men might be able to cope satisfactorily with her, but he was not one of them. He did not understand her, but even if he did, would that be any better?

Why pick on me? he thought plaintively. There must be dozens of men around free and glad to marry her; why had they not done so? Was it simply that he had been the first suitable one to appear in the district? And why was she so anxious for it? Was it "sex"? He dismissed that as absurd. Was it because she was lonely? Well, maybe. Was it for status? He tossed himself about the bed; he wished he could grasp the elements of understanding women. Many men knew exactly what women were about; some men fancied themselves as being expert in the interpretation of a woman's many facets; others believed them merely one-sided.

When it had come to the question of his own marriage, there had been no problem; he saw his beloved and he loved her at once, thought did not enter into it, it had been a matter of pure instinct; he did not even have to make a formal request to her to marry him, she had fallen into his

20

hands like a ripe plum that he had stretched up to pick, and they had lived happily, alas, not forever after. He rolled over and with his head upon his arms, he wept, not for himself but for her, because she had gone, gone, gone forever, and there were not many nights in the past nine years when he had not wept because gone is gone.

After a long time he said aloud into the dark and the silence: "I'll go." He meant that he would accept the FO's offer and go to the Trucial States. He would go because he wanted to, *he wanted to*. Why not? The boys would not care whether he went or not, they hated him, or so he thought, in the way one thinks at three o'clock in the morning. It seemed that the more he did for them, the more they did not love him. They had never loved him. They loved each other but not him. His mother would come to look after them but not willingly; she would not grumble, she was an old stoic, but she would come unsmiling as one marching forward staunchly to perform a duty.

He would go because he needed to be reinstated within himself; with the ruling sheikhs he never put a foot wrong, he knew where he was even without thinking; there was never a doubt in his mind whether he should or should not make this or that decision—it came naturally.

He gave a great sigh and tossed himself over so that the bed creaked in protest. What a relief it would be never again to set eyes upon his persecutor even at the cost of never seeing how his plants were doing. Even at the cost of having to telephone to the garage bloke asking him to bring the pickup back from the station and drive the Rolls-Royce back to its owner, on the dot of eight o'clock, when he, the mechanic, arrived at work. The money he would lose by ceasing to work on the Furnish estate would be covered, for the time being, by his payment from the FO. The future would have to look after itself; something would turn up.

The stair creaked; he lay holding his breath in order to hear the creak which would follow from the last step but one, if anybody were coming upstairs. He heard it, and two more which meant that two pairs of feet were coming upstairs. He heard nothing more.

So what had they been doing?

Had they been out?

The wry thought that they might have already been courting flashed across his mind, but was dismissed as obscene. Cinematic sex instruction they had been having at school in the biology lesson; he knew this because he had eavesdropped: he had listened to their raucous laughter as they repeated to each other the particular gems that had amused them, as two small boys might have repeated to one another the lusty jokes they had heard from the vulgar comic at a pantomime. He remembered Joshua, evidently intent on something, bringing the conversation to an end with an old-fashioned: "Oh, my sakes! What a carry-on!" and the final disgusted contempt from James: "The silly fools, as if we didn't know!"

So what had they been doing away from their beds well after midnight?

The creaking stair was no lullaby; he still could not sleep. As he lay thinking over and over the ghastly scene in the Furnish kitchen, he felt his face burning in the dark: the shame and ignominy of it all. He could never face her again, and here they were, practically neighbors, bound to meet from time to time at parties, as he started to know more people in the district. Though he had loved the Middle East he was glad to be "home," settled in his own dear land. And now within two years he had messed things up, rendered for himself someone living nearby with whom he was not on speaking terms.

It was intolerable, and he became worked up, sweaty with irritation and frustration in the way that happens between 2 and 4 A.M. With the first cool glimmer of greenish dawn he cooled down, he lay on his back, inert, and waited for sleep, which did not come till seven o'clock and lasted less than an hour.

He heard the postman lean his bicycle against the big iron gates of the drive and walk across to the lodge; he heard the letters or bills flutter into the tiny hall.

He had been going to fetch his small Yorkshire terrier bitch home from the kennels today where she had been for three weeks while in season. He would telephone the kennels after he had rung up about the car and ask them to keep her for the time he was away. He would not go and say good-bye to her, it hurt too much; she was as happy there as any little dog could be in a kennel, since it was where she had been born, but she much preferred being with him, going to work with him in the greenhouse, remaining gummed to his heels all day and sleeping on his bed all night.

And suddenly he went to sleep again.

4

The next thing was this curious scraping sound which brought him wide awake and told him it was after nine: Mrs. Flower was brushing the handmade rugs. He smiled, remembering the little struggle he had had with her, since brushing carpets had seemed to her the most archaic activity she had heard of, on a par with carrying milk pails on a yoke. Only three out of his precious collection of rugs would fit into the living room on the floor, and he had had to have the little house cheaply carpeted to make it tolerably comfortable. The furniture was of the most rickety and inconsiderable. He had explained to Mrs. Flower at boring length that his rugs had been the collection of a lifetime, handmade and ancient, and must on no account be vacuumed, the three being used on the floor had to be hand-swept. Some hung on the wall, and the remainder were in store. He listened to her slavish activity apathetically, only half-awake. Then he sprang out of bed, remembering the telephoning he had to do.

It was Saturday; there was some sort of athletic activity at the school this morning about which the boys had told him. A bus was leaving the village for those who wished to go; to judge by the lack of other sounds in the house, they had gone.

He was annoyed that he had overslept because he

needed the pickup for the Saturday morning shopping; the Rolls still stood outside in the drive. Shaved and dressed, he went downstairs and at once telephoned to the garage to fetch the pickup from the station. He spent no more time on speculating about his decision during the night; he dialed again.

"Is that you, Frank? Buzz here. It's on."

"That's fine, Buzz! I was pretty sure you were not going to play."

"I thought it over. I had a white night about it, I may say."

"I think you've made the right decision, old man. It won't pay off acting the wet nurse to those two young thugs of yours . . ." but one could hear the smile in his voice.

Arrangements were made for the departure. Then he telephoned to his mother.

"Yes, dear boy, of course I will come. Next week?"

"Good old Mum. I'll get my room spring-cleaned and have the drawers emptied. Can you manage Monday?"

"The day after tomorrow?" Slight pause. "I'll try."

"Oh, Mum, I am grateful to you for this . . . if you come on Monday I'll be here for two nights, put up the camp bed in the sitting room for myself, there's only two bedrooms, you'll remember. I'll have time to show you the ropes and go up to town on Thursday, leaving on Friday. Bless you. . . ."

Thinking back, later, he knew that if he had gone straight into the kitchen and set about making his coffee, he would have remembered. But after putting down the receiver, he picked up the mail and pulled the *Times* from where it hung halfway through the letter box. Riveted by the day's bad news, reading it, he went into the living room and sat down, still reading. What would the leader say about this? He turned to the middle page to see. He read the leader, he read the rest of the page, including the readers' letters, and Mrs. Flower came in to say there was a young man from the garage, he had brought the pickup from the station and wanted the key of the Rolls.

"It's in the car, Mrs. Flower." No, he hadn't taken the key out; he had been so upset on his return he did not care whether an attempt was made to steal the car or not.

"The key's in it," he snarled, as she hesitated.

"Mrs. Flower!" he called as she closed the front door. "I want you a minute." He told her he was going abroad on a job and that he had asked his mother to come. Mrs. Flower had seen old Mrs. Patricott and approved of her. She said it was quite all right as far as she was concerned and she was glad he was going to have a "bit of a change." In her opinion it would do the boys good to be "on their own," and he understood that what she meant by "on their own" was . . . without him.

He always felt unaccountably uncomfortable sitting in his armchair when Mrs. Flower was standing. He stood up, his behind to the empty grate, hands behind his back.

"The boys were terribly upset yesterday when they got home from school," Mrs. Flower said. "Someone's shot their girl, no, I mean hen pigeon or whatever you call it."

"Well, well!" he exclaimed as though he did not already know.

"Looks like they might be right, there was blood. . . ."

"Where is it?" he exclaimed.

Mrs. Flower hid the irresistible smile that appeared on her face, behind her hand. "They buried her, with knobs on . . ." she added, meaning with some ceremony, since they had told her they had taken the sock for a "winding sheet."

"Where was she found?"

"Beside their loft, lying on the ground."

"But you were here yesterday morning, weren't you? You would have heard a shot?"

"Not when I'm brushing I wouldn't."

There was a lack of understanding between them on this subject, so there was an uncomfortable little pause after she mentioned it.

"The trouble is," Mrs. Flower said reluctantly and with sad eyes, "they think you dunnit. They achewally think you shot their bird!"

"Why me?" he asked patiently.

"Don't ask me, they've got some funny ideas about you, those kids."

"Where are they now?"

Mrs. Flower jerked her head, indicating that they had gone up to the house to see their friend Mr. O'Duff. "I know they ought to have caught the school bus this morning for some games stunt, but they were off before I had time to say anything; they were gone when I had my coat hung up!" She added: "Sir." She did this only when she felt sorry for him and when she was really thinking what she was saying. Otherwise, as often as not, she called him "Love."

"I was in town yesterday, as you know. I ran the boys down to the school bus on my way to the station and I wasn't back till . . . till late, long after their bedtime."

Oh, hell! That damned woman Desirée! He had had no right to go off for the rest of the evening with her; the fact that he had not wanted to was neither here nor there. It was his job to come home and be with the boys. The sickening disgust of himself that he had constantly to fight back flowed over him as it did several times a week. No wonder his boys despised him; he was a weak fool. And was it surprising that they crept out during the night or in the very early hours? He had not the foggiest idea what they might have been doing, but he spent more time condemning himself than in speculation.

He had never taken the boys to a psychiatrist, but he had sneaked off to one to discuss, not himself, but his relationship with his sons. It appeared that he was the *fons et origo mali* as far as his boys went, and that loosely translated meant that he was "the root of all evil," a diagnosis discouraging to any attempts to fraternize with them.

He went into the kitchen and made himself coffee *his* way, shuddering with disgust at the thought of an electric percolator which had certainly not prevented him from drinking a lot too much coffee last night.

The kitchen and dining room being one and the same, with benches round the plastic-topped table, he sat at the table and stirred his coffee while Mrs. Flower banged about in his bedroom above. He remembered the half pie in his dispatch case, and rising to fetch it from the hall, he received a piercing stab of memory full in the midriff, as it were, which slung him back onto the bench with his head in his hands.

The dispatch case was in Desirée's hall; in his wounded exit last night, he had forgotten it. Wounded is the correct word because he felt, indeed, morally wounded; it was not the abuse that had been so wounding but the anguish of witnessing such a major loss of self-control on the part of his hostess, it hurt him beyond words to see other people so . . . as he thought it . . . *dégorgé-ing* themselves. Back again in the repetitive recitation of last night's thoughts, he reminded himself that not only did he never want to see her again, he took it for granted that she would find it unbearable ever to face him again, and that was what had decided him, much against his will, never to "set foot" again in her greenhouses. He was in no doubt at all that she would understand his nonappearance.

Mrs. Flower bustled in with some soiled linen, which she pushed into the washing machine: "What's up, love?"

"Nothing at all," he returned fiercely, stirring his coffee.

"What about your little Maggie?"

"I'm just going to ring the kennels and ask them to keep her another three weeks; it's the only answer. It isn't that I feel you won't look after her splendidly, Mrs. Flower, but I'm frightened about someone leaving the little gate open."

There were big wrought-iron gates to the drive entrance, but the traffic to and from the big house was such that they were kept permanently open, and the brigadier had had permission from Mr. O'Duff to have a wooden fence and small gate put up entirely round the lodge and the scrap of garden. The reason he gave to Mrs. Flower for not having the little terrier back while he was away might have been *a* reason, but it was not *the* reason, which was that he knew Maggie was reasonably happy, if not in ecstasy, at the kennels and that if she came home and he were not there, she would be suicidally cast down (except that dogs simply stay totally miserable with no escape to oblivion).

"Perhaps it's for the best," Mrs. Flower agreed.

Having finished his breakfast, he told her he was now going out shopping, asked her for her list of requirements, and as he got up and went to the hall, the telephone rang.

He lifted the receiver: "It's Wilf from the garridge."

"Oh, yes?"

"I'm at the Red House, sir."

"Where?" Desirée's house, he remembered.

"I'm just waiting for the van to pick me up from the garridge. The police is all over the place, there's been a nasty raid in the night here, the place is all topsy-turvy. . . ."

The brigadier sprang to attention, as it were, as he always did at the faintest sign of an emergency, his brain now working with efficiency. His first thought was to get his dispatch case back, not because of the half pie, of course, but because he had to have it for the trip to the Middle East and he wanted it now.

But Wilf was breathless, partly from fear, perhaps, but a great deal more from the pleasure of passing on really shocking news. "The old girl . . ." he spluttered in his excitement, "she's dead, she's a goner, been bumped off, so they tell me, I mean her cleaning woman tells me, she's in hysterics, I just been pouring brandy down her throat . . ." and his own, it would seem, at the same time.

"Just a minute, just a minute . . . what old girl?"

"Mrs. Thingamejig, Mrs. What's-her-name, Mrs. Who's-it?"

"Pull yourself together, Wilf!"

"The lady of the house, I can't remember her name."

"Do you mean . . . Mrs. Furnish, Wilf?"

"That's right!"

The brigadier appeared to be gagging himself with his hand.

"Are you there, sir? Eh? I say, are you *there?*"

"Yes, I'm here, Wilf, I'm just surprised, that's all."

"I thought you would be, is why I gave you a tinkle, just so's you'd be not too shocked when they come."

"Come where?"

"To you."

"The police?"

"That's right. They'll want to know what I was doing with the Rolls, won't they? And you'll be able to tell them, eh? I don't want to be under any kind of shadder, see. . . ."

"Of course not, Wilf. Don't worry. I'll put that right."

"They'll want to know what *you* was doing with the Rolls, sir. They didn't exactly ask me, but I knew that's what they was thinking."

He paused before answering: "It's just what I'm wondering myself. Are you there, Wilf? They don't need to come, I'll be along when I can; I work there."

"Oh, I see, you *work* here." His informant was clearly mystified.

"She came to the station to meet me off the train, we had some business about the hothouse to discuss, that is why my pickup was left at the station."

"I see . . ." but he seemed disinclined to ring off.

"I've a spot of weekend shopping to do first, and I'll be right along, within the hour. Tell the dicks, will you?"

That was a good one; he poured himself more coffee, but his hand was shaking, and when he sat down again at the table, his face seemed to have shrunk.

5

Mr. O'Duff's at the top of the drive was a pleasant old Queen Anne house, but it looked dead from the front—all the windows had their shutters closed; at a close look you could see how the front door seemed to be roped shut with cobwebs. One or two sections of the roof pediment were missing. There were shallow steps up to the front door, and on either side those half windows appearing above the ground from gratings which give the impression of a house straining upward to pull itself completely out of the ground. As with un-lived-in houses the outside peeling paint on the woodwork around the windows was almost showy, as though the house were crying for help.

O'Duff, reported to be a rich man, had lived there all of ten years and had never done any maintenance whatever. His father had come from Ireland during Hitler's war and had opened a small garage in the village. Owing possibly to the nearby presence of an American garrison, he became quickly successful, helped by his son who served the gasoline. When he died, the son had sold up and bought the dower house, half a mile from the village, built himself a magnificent pigeon loft in the old stable block and devoted himself to the Fancy. He lived reasonably comfortably in the kitchen premises, with the old servants' hall for a bedroom and the larder for his surplus store of birds' food. They consumed an immense amount of food to judge by the trucks and vans which came up the quarter-mile drive, swinging around the yard and delivering their crates and cases.

"Food," he told the boys, "is the most important thing about this game; feed your bird right and it will repay you all along the line. It's not that there's much more to it than common sense . . ." but he seemed entirely oblivious of this when it came to his own intake, because it would seem that he lived in the main upon tinned baked beans, oven-baked potatoes and fried bacon and eggs, nice in themselves but not exactly suitable for every meal. The old kitchen garden, behind the stables, surrounded by a delightful, warm-looking brick wall, was entirely neglected except for a couple of square yards where he grew such green stuffs as he gave the pigeons, mainly lettuce.

He had finished his baked-bean breakfast when the boys arrived and was sitting in his rocking chair, his feet up on the stove, reading the *Daily Mirror*. He had black hair, straggling across his forehead, and a pixielike, long, pointed face with a long nose which clung to his face flatly rather than sticking out; his mouth was unusually thin and mobile so that he seemed often upon the edge of laughter when the boys were there. His eyes were the color of a goat's, a Celtic face if ever there was one, and in all his forty-or-so years he had shed not all of his Irish accent, with the old saws like "Bedad!" and "Begorrah!" which should all have died a decent death long ago. He seemed to do it deliberately, as though thrusting at you the fact that he was an Irishman of the deepest dye.

But he had a rough edge to his tongue, and the brigadier would say that he wouldn't trust him any farther than he could kick him, but there were times when he would croon gently some song from his homeland in a way which would draw tears from a stone. He also had a tiresomely jokey way of talking, leaving you in some doubt whether or not he was serious.

Though doubtless surprised that the boys should have called on him unusually early, he gave no trace of it, he did not even look up from his folded newspaper.

"Hi, fellers!"

They had ceased long ago to call him "Mr. O'Duff," at his own request. "You call me Duffer, because that's what I am, when all's said and done," he had said, and they had succeeded in thus addressing him after a short struggle.

"You've come to tell me about your grand squeakers!" meaning the young from newly hatched eggs.

The boys exchanged glances; which was to tell him? Joshua nudged James. "We haven't," James croaked. "The hen's dead!"

Mr. O'Duff let his feet fall from the stove with a crash, and swung his rocking chair around to face them. "You're joking!"

Joshua shook his head dumbly, and James, looking down at his feet, as stricken and ashamed as though himself were guilty, said: "She was shot!"

"Wait a minute, wait a minute. . . ."

"It's true." Joshua nodded miserably.

"What divil would have done that?" Mr. O'Duff flung down his newspaper as dramatically as though casting a hand grenade. "Are you sure, man?"

Between them they described the purple-scarlet wound, the open staring eyes, the cool feathers, the stiffness. They told how they had been so completely sure they had hurried her into the ground, sick at the sight. But there had been no doubt at all, she was murdered.

"And Father was in town, he took us to the bus on his way to the station, so we know he *went*, but . . ." Joshua started, but Mr. O'Duff squashed that line of talk in no uncertain terms. He had had to deal with this father phobia in the boys before; he never delayed his sarcastic abuse of them.

31

They received the reprobation in silence, but with set lips and determined expressions until it was over.

"What about Maggie; why didn't she scare the living daylights out of the intruder?" he asked, when he had finished his reproval.

"Maggie is in season, she's been at the kennels three weeks. . . ."

"We *told* you: the hen was shot and Mrs. Flower didn't hear anything. But she goes early in the weekdays when we're at school."

"I can't believe it, I can't credit anyone would do such a wicked thing, a lovely bird . . . who would want to shoot her?"

"We can't dig her up to prove to you . . ." James said in a choking voice.

"We're not dotty," Joshua put in, "we know when somebody's been *shot!*"

Mr. O'Duff sat back in his chair, and biting his thumb, he began musing: "Friday morning, now what monster would want to go out shooting on a Friday morning, I ask meself?" He was asking himself as an old-fashioned Catholic, who fasted on a Friday. Not, perhaps, entirely irrelevant, pigeon flesh might be acceptable as fast food. He frowned, playing with his lips; pressing them together with his fingers, he looked at the boys to see if they had received the message. James had; Joshua was still looking distraught and wretched.

"I'm afraid," Mr. O'Duff said steadily, "it may have been one of those rich, retired louts living in one of those new twenty-thousand-pound houses on the new estate. One of those respectable folk, out for a morning's sport like a real gent. He wouldn't know the difference between a racing pigeon and a pig's arse. . . ."

As always in their Duffer's beneficent aura, they began to cheer up.

"God rot him," Mr. O'Duff went on darkly. "I wonder which one of them fat buggers it was? I'll go along and knock his teeth down his throat when I've made sure; I don't want to half kill the wrong chap, eh?"

They revived visibly.

"But the cock's looking after the kids, I mean, squeakers," Joshua piped excitedly.

"There's the boy!" Mr. O'Duff responded delightedly. "Their dad will save the squeakers; fathers do come in useful at times!"

Since the hen bird's egg-sitting stint ends at 10 A.M. varying only very slightly, the cock bird, in fact, should have taken over anyway, but Mr. O'Duff did not remind them of that; what he was worrying about was how the cock could be helped in the task that both pigeons carry out with great dedication: the mutual task of feeding the newly hatched squabs for their first three weeks.

He huddled himself up small in his rocking chair, frowned and pressed his fist to his lips: "Now, men, we've got to plan this campaign very carefully . . . we must bring up reinforcements. We must rally round the young father, willing as he may be, there's a limit to what a young man can do; you can't rock the cradle and milk the cow at one and the same time . . . and yet"—he gave a short bark of laughter at the ridiculous suggestion—"you can't replace his hen by another without he knows, not by a long chalk. He loved that girl; he's a sorrowing widder man. We'll have to find him a mother's help." He leaned forward, scowling horribly. *"But will he take to her?* . . . That's the problem."

The population enjoyed calling it "the village," but the actual village was an acre or two in the center of the conurbation: the church and graveyard around it, the almshouses, the rectory, some self-conscious new-old cottages standing in a row, and the rest was restoration and new building, including supermarket, rejuvenated pub and the garage, unrecognizable as the original establishment but still called *B. O'Duff and Son.*

The brigadier, carrying his basket, made his first call at the garage. Just this once his orders had been carried out immediately; he knew why. Wilf liked driving the Rolls more than anything on earth, and there had no doubt been a short sharp struggle between the two mechanics as to which would drive the other to pick it up and which would drive the Rolls back to its owner.

He was irritated: all this ridiculous picking up and to-ing and fro-ing simply because he had given in to the damned woman; it was like rubbing salt into the sore, but if there had been a breaking in and entering at the house, not to mention a murder, every small movement of cars and of Buzz Patricott himself would be of significance. So he simply confirmed that someone pick up Wilf from the Red House, and saying nothing else he stalked into the self-service store and started to put purchases straight into his own basket instead of into one of the wire baskets provided.

Like one in a dream he put lard, margarine, butter, bread, a shoulder of New Zealand lamb . . . cheese . . . into his basket, but he was not thinking of dead Mrs. Furnish, oddly enough. He was thinking about the open flap of a tent through which he saw the sand floor covered with glowing gems of rugs; dark, dark, handsome, dignified faces below . . . serving girls with beautiful hands . . . a daydream of the Trucial State to which he might be bound.

The girl at the cash desk snatched the box of brown eggs from him as he stood turning it dreamily over and over: "That'll be two hundred and ten pence, Colonel," she snapped, piling everything back in his basket. "Next, please."

Would this trouble at the Red House mean he could not go? he asked himself as, with sightless eyes, he walked across to the garage. Would he have to put it all off to "help the police with their inquiries"?

It had never paid him, he mused, to do what he *wanted*, not that he had *wanted* to go back home after dinner with Desirée, but he must have thought it an acceptable idea; otherwise he would not have complied. He must have thought gin and tonic in a comfortable bar preferable to arriving home to kippers and two sulky youngsters. He mused bitterly upon his bad luck in happening to do what was more pleasant upon that particular evening. It was a matter of his inherent bad luck. He brooded, as he so often did, upon being a left-handed person; he was a sinistral, a wise woman of the East had once told him, like a spiral seashell she had shown him, the whorls of which went to

34

the left instead of to the right like all the others. His was the left, or dark, side of the shield, she had said. Napoleon had been so intelligent, he thought, as he sat on the small dainty wall fronting the garage, waiting for service, so acute that he asked when choosing his generals: "Is he lucky?"

He, Basil, was not lucky and perhaps that was why the boys did not like him. The more he tried to please them the less successful he was. It must be a matter of luck; maybe he was born to be unpleasing rather than pleasing, he was perhaps truly sinistral, that was maybe why he had been passed over when they were promoting to top rank. That could be why his beloved had died young . . . but now he had gone too far, into the realms of pure absurdity; he shook himself mentally, almost as a dog does, but in a human being it appears as a slight shudder from head to foot.

The drive in front of the Red House was packed; there was no room for the pickup which had to be parked out of sight of the house, against the rhododendrons. There was the Rolls, a big Rover police car, two small local mini-cars with blue lights on the roof and POLICE written large, and . . . and there was the ambulance, large and white and almost new, a gift from the ladies of the county. Desirée herself, he remembered, had had a coffee morning in aid of funds to buy this new ambulance. Was she really lying mangled inside it?

He went around the side of the house, to the greenhouse, His Place.

There were things to be watered and in the pleasant warmth he filled the can, remembering, as he sprinkled the sweet-smelling plants, a number of practical facts that had to be considered.

For one thing, his fingerprints in the house would be everywhere, on the glasses, the coffee table, the cigarette box which he had taken from his hostess . . . in the kitchen on the Formica-topped table, the coffee cups, the spoon, the sugar jar . . . the stools they had pulled out from under the table.

The foul abuse she had thrown at him, for him would hang in the air like mobiles, but fortunately they would not be visible to others. They were there, all the same, too vulgar to be remembered.

Ugh! Was he going to have to tell the police some of that?

Quaint anachronisms like "an officer and a gentleman" flashed across his awareness to be suppressed instantly. But he thought over carefully a suitable description: "We had a disagreement." No, that wouldn't do. What was the disagreement about? The stools were knocked over, the milk bottle had rolled off the table onto the floor, the electric coffee percolator, its flex stretched from the dresser to the table, wrenched from its socket and in smithereens on the tiled floor. . . .

Had she left everything as it was and staggered off to bed, hurt?

Or had she recovered sufficiently to tidy up before retiring?

Had the thieves been outside among the rhododendrons observing the terrible scene in the lighted kitchen through the unblinded windows? Or had they come later when the doors had been firmly locked and the lights turned out after his departure?

Had they been simply reconnoitering? Making plans for a raid another night but, seeing the present chaos, deciding upon immediate action? Or action a few hours later when she had gone to bed and, probably, to sleep?

Staring down at his seedling petunias, Buzz Patricott heard the heavy footsteps of the law approaching. He squared his shoulders and turned to the door, chin up and hands straight down on either side, as he would stand to face a firing squad.

It was a cleaning woman, letting herself in with her key at eight o'clock, who had to describe the scene, though in fact she had touched nothing. The kitchen was tidy but the smashed milk bottle and the broken percolator had been brushed into a dustpan and left on the floor beside the back door.

The coffee cups were in the sink, unwashed, the stools standing neatly under the table. The hall light was on, the drawing-room door stood half-open; the owner of the house was sitting on the sofa, in front of the electric fire, which was still on. She appeared from behind to be sitting perfectly normally at one end of the high sofa, and Mrs. Mop had walked across the floor to her, saying: "Whatever are you doing there, ma'am?" Peering anxiously at her from the front, she believed Mrs. Furnish to be seriously ill (no, she did not think her lady drunk) because her head was lolling sideways against the high side of the settee, her hands upon her lap. She did not touch her but picked up the telephone beside the fireplace, fumbled through the damask-covered booklet of local telephone numbers and dialed the doctor. One of the partners came within ten minutes, during which Mrs. Mop discovered that her lady was dead, there being no movement of breathing whatever and her hands almost cold.

Mrs. Mop believed her lady had died of a heart attack; she believed she had dined with friends because she was wearing a frock and jacket she often wore for dinner, and her mink jacket was hanging over the back of a chair near the door. She believed that she had eaten something which disagreed with her at dinner, on arriving home had not gone up to her bedroom but had turned on the drawing-room fire and sat down to recover from the pain in her chest, poor dear. That was her favorite seat on the weird old sofa, against the tall arm on the window side.

The doctor went into the drawing room by himself, with Mrs. Mop wringing her hands in the hall: it was not long before he came out and said that Mrs. Furnish had been shot in the head on the side against the sofa; on the left side, presumably and at a quick look, twice. Mrs. Mop was rendered speechless for quite a long time. She sat at the kitchen table, sipping some cooking brandy, which helped to calm her violent shuddering.

There was no kind local bobby around to make caustic comments to relieve the starkness. The county constabulary's crime squad zoomed in upon the scene, stern of purpose as commandos, with no meandering, the top brass like business executives. Their attitude was very faintly that they must hurry on with this lot, there were more important

37

things waiting to be attended to, and it looked very much as though they would have the whole thing wrapped up by lunchtime. Family murders bored them now; they could hardly be bothered with them; these were kept for the second and third rung of young rising detectives, while the top brass concerned themselves with assassinations (which had become much worse than ordinary murder), supra-local-and-suburban affairs, bank robberies, arson and things concerned with anarchy and bomb throwing. By midday they had the case neatly solved in their minds at least, leaving the final details to the younger men.

Facts are what matter in law, and the facts at the Red House were textbook in their simplicity. The benevolent protectress and the harried brigadier offered no problem at all other than the old Unsound Mind let-out. It was not necessarily *in cold blood*. Though the type of gun used had not yet been decided upon because the bullets were still inside the victim, it had been a small, neat, pocket affair. The brigadier had been in London all day and undoubtedly always carried a gun with him when he went to town, though he denied this of course. The drinks at the Woolstapler's Arms; the dinner afterward; the drive back to the Red House for coffee. The argument in the kitchen, about money, of course; the brigadier's anger; the return to the drawing room, where the argument continued. The bringing out of the gun and the shooting. All nice and clean and easy. No sex, well . . . probably not; no bashing up, no mess, no recrimination.

The brigadier stated curtly and quietly, without any visible emotion, what had happened at the Red House. He denied firmly having a gun with him at all. He kept one, of course, as any military man would; he would have no hesitation at all in showing it to them: *Charter Arms undercover .38 special*: a 16-oz. light revolver with a 5-shot cylinder. He had bought it in Beirut the year before last and had a British license for it.

If it had not been for the dispatch case in the hall, of course, with the royal arms on the flap, the brigadier would never have been suspected, because nobody would have known he was there, even if someone had remembered he

38

had been dining with her previously. No doubt there were a great many good sets of fingerprints, but then if people are not suspected, their fingerprints are not compared with those found on the scene of the crime. He simply said that his fingerprints would be found all over the place and there was no doubt that they would be.

Asked, finally, if he had shot Mrs. Furnish, he said no, he had not. He said it was difficult to shoot anybody without a weapon. He went on to say he knew that a motive could easily be drummed up; he had admitted to having had a pretty considerable row with the lady. But he had not shot her.

It was he who said that there were motives for it, but shooting was not the manner in which he would resolve this particular problem. He said that she had been kind to him in that she employed him at a reasonable salary to look after her considerable hothouse, that he had done so for about eighteen months, she giving him an absolutely free hand and he providing the house with all the grapes, tomatoes, cucumbers and hothouse flowers that they could use. She was generous, too, in allowing him to keep any profits from outside sales after all expenses in heating and materials were paid.

So what was the row about?

It had to come to that, and because the situation was so desperate he had to abandon all his principles of behavior. He said simply: "She wanted me to marry her."

"And you refused?"

He tried not to shuffle his feet and to show his discomfort. "It wasn't quite as cut-and-dried as that . . . there was no question of my marrying her; as far as I was concerned, there never had been. The benefits she outlined . . . did not outweigh the . . . the, er . . . the disadvantages. I've been married before, and I do not feel that any new marriage that has been mooted so far could come up to the one I enjoyed for so short a time in the Middle East."

He was leaving in the pickup, having told them that the Rolls's steering wheel would show plenty of his fingerprints. It was too early in the proceedings for an arrest or even for detaining for questioning, but he felt that the trip

39

to the Middle East at the beginning of the next week was off; that was quite obvious. To clear out now would be to damn himself to outer darkness. Though he could have done some more work in the greenhouse—he would have liked to plant his begonia corms this morning—Mrs. Flower would be waiting for the household purchases, murder or no murder.

He drove home slowly and thoughtfully. He could see no way out of this; he knew very little about the woman, on the whole, but this murder smacked of one of those ancient crime books where the murderer is found to be some relative, abandoned baby son from thirty years ago, maybe; cousin from the outback who has been harboring revenge all these years; long-lost heir to the Furnish fortunes . . . the list was endless.

"She hadn't an enemy in the world!" people were bound to say; she was a do-gooder of the first order and as generous as generous people can be; respectability was her banner, there was nothing nasty in the woodshed of her impeccable existence.

But there must have been, since somebody went very late at night into her drawing room, somebody she must have known, since the front door was this morning found to be unlocked, though all the downstairs windows were fastened for the night. She had good watercolors on the walls, real silver on the dining-room sideboard, excellent furniture, valuable rings on her fingers, real pearls round her neck, and these were all untouched by the intruder, nor were they of the quality which will attract the new-style educated burglar.

Back home the milkman was driving away as the brigadier turned into the drive and parked on the grass verge, so he knew that Mrs. Flower would, absolutely certainly, have heard the news from him if not from anybody else during the morning. He wondered where the boys were. He carried the basket inside, and Mrs. Flower came out of the kitchen, holding her hand out for the basket.

"Poor you!" she started. "I've heard all about it. Burglars, was it? Poor woman . . . she didn't deserve that!"

"Where are the boys?"

"Up at the house, have been all morning."

"Well, we'll be having lunch late, Mrs. Flower, so I have time to telephone to London to put off my mother and my trip. . . ."

"So you won't be going!"

"I can't. I'm number one suspect, Mrs. Flower."

After a moment's pause Mrs. Flower laughed, she actually laughed. "Go on!"

"It's true, I was ass enough not to come straight home after I was in town. I went out to dinner with Mrs. Furnish and afterwards we went back to her house to make coffee"—he said this eyeing her sternly—"we had a bit of a row, as a matter of fact, a disagreement, the police call it, and I left in a hurry, leaving my dispatch case on a chair in the hall. So I've been talking to the police for a long time, 'helping them in their inquiries,' it's called. Ever heard that before?"

Mrs. Flower was now staring at him in horror. She gave a big swallow and said: "You don't really mean. . . ."

"I do. . . ."

He went to the telephone, leaving Mrs. Flower gaping.

". . . well, Mother, the fact is there's been a bit of bother down here. A woman I know, I dined with her last night, has been shot. I said *shot!* No, I didn't, dear! Well, I can't go away because I'll have to attend the inquest and all that . . . well, Mother dear, I knew you'd be glad to be relieved of the responsibility of the boys . . . yes, of course we'll keep you posted."

He could now have made a personal call to Sir Frank Ansdell's house in Surrey, but instead he rang up the Foreign Office: there was always somebody there, even at the weekends, and left the message to be relayed at once to all those concerned that Brigadier Patricott was obliged to cancel his trip to the Middle East next week owing to matters beyond his control.

Frank would ring back, of course, as soon as he received the message, but he would be out; he could not, he simply could not face a lengthy explanation yet. He could hardly bear to think about it, let alone talk about it on the telephone. Blow hot, blow cold, yes, I'll go, no, I won't go.

Would Ansdell think that the friend who had always been slightly eccentric had now finally—

"I'm going for Maggie, Mrs. Flower . . ." he shouted, trying to get out of the front door without seeing her, but she came rushing out of the kitchen.

"There's no need for you to worry, Brigadier love, no need at all."

He paused out of politeness, hand on the partly open door. "How do you make that out, Mrs. Flower?"

"She's a magistrate . . . or was, I mean Mrs. Furnish."

He stared blankly at her: "How does that help?"

"It helps a lot, don't you see?"

"No, I don't!"

"She was chairman of the magistrates for a bit. . . ."

"I still don't see. . . ."

Mrs. Flower shook her head sadly, as though dealing with a backward child. "Well, I could of easily shot her myself if I'd had a gun, that time our Freddy and a friend of his was had up before them for breaking teacher's window . . . they treated it like it was a crime!"

He clicked his tongue, shocked. "Really, Mrs. Flower!"

Carried away, she went on in an unusual way for her: "They're not like judges, they's only ordinary folk like usselves, yet the way they carry on you'd think they was God. There's lots of folk ony need a gun . . . they've bumped one or two of them off long afore now. . . ."

"Mrs. Flower, you really mustn't, you really must not . . . I'm just off to fetch my Maggie home!" He closed the front door quietly behind him and made a dash for the pickup before she could continue her discourse.

He was back with Maggie, and the smell of the roast mutton was welcoming. He was glad, too, to hear that the boys were back from wherever they had been. It was quite clear from the sounds they were making that they knew nothing about what had been happening, and as he sat down and squeezed Maggie, still on his knees, under the table, he realized, with sinking heart, that it would be he who would have to tell them. The boys clattered in, took their places at table and acknowledged the presence of their father quite cheerfully, out of habit, he supposed. Maggie pushed her moplike head up and received a great welcome from Joshua.

He plunged in without thinking what he was going to say; so often he thought carefully what words he would use when being serious with the boys, and whatever he chose was not a success, so he gave up trying.

"Your friend Mrs. Furnish is dead. . . ." There was a startled pause. Mrs. Flower was draining "her" cabbage at the sink, enveloped in steam, her pale hair hanging either side of her face wispily.

They both spoke at once. One of the boys said: "Good!" overenthusiastically, and the other said: "Who killed her?" And Joshua pulled Maggie out and hugged her, whispering, "Thank goodness," into her tousled hair.

"Now shut up!" their father said irritably. "It's serious. I was with her till nearly midnight, and because they want me for the inquest and so on I've had to cancel the trip. . . ."

Staring fixedly at the joint of meat which Mrs. Flower now laid in front of the brigadier, Joshua asked: "What were you doing with her till nearly midnight?"

It was that kind of thing that threw the brigadier, he did not know how to cope with it; this loathsome knowingness in his two small sons broke not only his heart but his will to try any longer. And right at the back of thought lay the hideous suspicion that though he loved them, he disliked them.

Mrs. Flower was on excellent terms with the boys, a condition of light banter, but when she was cross with them and disapproved, she went stony-faced and silent, enveloping herself in a cold, gray cloud from which it took a good deal of tact to release her. In spite of the savory meal she had prepared, she did this now, sitting down and staring ahead of her over the vegetable dishes which she banged down in front of them. She did not get up to get gravy either, and the boys had to help with the serving. The brigadier carved sitting down and every now and then two pricked ears and a minute black button of a nose appeared over the tabletop. Nobody could ever see Maggie's eyes; a veil of creamy-silver, indeed more than a veil, a curtain hung between those great shining orbs and the world. She was doing her best to relieve the ghastly silence that had fallen upon her people. But this time nobody took any notice.

After he had eaten his plateful of food James sat back and said that though it would be lovely without her, he was sorry for that old bird Desirée. Joshua would have said that *he wasn't* were it not for the forbidding atmosphere. But fed, everyone relaxed, and discussion started with the brigadier telling them that someone had broken in or been let into the house after he had left and had shot her in the head as she sat on the big knowle settee; they had shot twice to make sure. The police were looking for the weapon, but what a hope! The boys asked if there had been a robbery, and the brigadier told them it was not yet decided; Mrs. Furnish's daughter was married to an American businessman living in San Francisco, and when he had left the Red House this morning, they were still waiting to get her on the telephone. "I don't think she was on good terms with her daughter," he remembered. So for a while, when the baked apples were eaten, they sat around the table like an ordinary family and, as he did every Saturday, the brigadier asked his sons what they would like to do this afternoon.

Sometimes they went to the cinema, but these occasions were becoming more rare since now there were nearly always films with titles like *The Body* or *Love Variations*. In a way into which their father did not inquire, the boys got into these X films on their own, but after the first three or four declared they found them deadly dull, and mysteriously, "only for the kids." They went eagerly to see an all-too-seldom cowboy film.

The brigadier always knew what he would like to do, which was drive, near or far, to a garden center or a hothouse of note, sometimes to the gardens of big houses open to the public, and mooch around thoughtfully, planning what he could or could not afford to have.

"It's a pity I have had to cancel the FO trip," he said. "The dibs I would have earned would have given us all a treat of some kind; there might have been enough to buy a secondhand Land-Rover to replace the pickup."

"You go, Father . . ." James urged, while under the table Joshua's foot shot out and aimed a sharp kick at his brother's shin at which James' well-meaning advice was blurred in an involuntary "Ow!"

Mrs. Flower liked to go early on Saturday so that she could give her own kitchen "a good red-up" for the weekend. She would not reappear until Monday; Sunday's lunch would consist of cold mutton and baked potatoes which she had scrubbed and left in readiness to go into the oven. The boys helped to clear away and wash up, then announced that they were going to give their loft "a good red-up, too."

The brigadier gathered up Maggie and the *Times,* with which he went into the sitting room, and then called the boys.

"What were you doing last night, or rather early this morning?" He was holding the newspaper and glancing at the front page in order to make his question lighter. He made a point of never asking what they were doing or had done. But this time it had to be. "Now look," he said, "I'm not snooping, but this time you've got to tell me; everyone who knew Mrs. Furnish well is going to have to account for themselves over the period during which she was killed. Whether or not they had anything to do with it they are liable to be questioned, not necessarily because they are suspect but because it might make them remember some incident that would have some bearing on the crime. So come on, boys, what were you doing?"

They were reasonable, he would say that for them. He would have smiled if he had dared, so gloriously innocent were their movements.

They told it between them: They had gone to their farmer friend nearby, "after tea" (meaning the kipper meal) "since you didn't come back home," and they had told him about the shooting of their hen pigeon, shot, presumably, in the turnover period when the father and mother pigeons changed places in the home and had "a bit of a fly around."

The farmer had kindly come up with a piece of wire and

an old battery outfit for electrifying the wire and had fixed up a protection around their pigeon loft; anyone approaching the loft to do any damage would receive a nasty little shock. It would hardly prevent further shooting but was a comforting gesture. They had been asleep some time when their father came in, but his entry had awakened them and they had decided, when all was quiet again, to creep out and make sure the rickety affair was working properly.

It was one of those rare occasions when father and sons were friends, equals, and the brigadier became inordinately lighthearted suddenly.

"Well, buzz off," he said, opening his newspaper, "I need a bit of a shut-eye after the shocks of this morning. You do what you want; maybe I'll think up something to do after tea."

The *Times* was over his face and a faint sound of snoring came from behind it as the huge yellow Cadillac passed the lodge windows. Only Maggie noticed it, sitting on his knees, half-covered by the newspaper. She raised her head and sniffed significantly.

6

Sherbia, the Sheikh of Janhara, leaned forward and tapped on the shoulder of the undergraduate of Keele University who was acting chauffeur during his vacation and motioned that he would like him to get out and do whatever was required to attract attention at the front door of the closely shuttered house. This the young man did, leaping out and pressing his finger on the front-door bell, stiff and dry. He shook his head demonstratively to indicate to the sheikh that the bell must be broken. "No ring!" he shouted.

The sheikh leaned back and held the lower part of his long blue-gray face with an equally long, blue-gray hand. "Again, encore!" he instructed.

Around the corner of the house came Mr. O'Duff. He was wearing a dirty white boiler suit and carrying an empty bucket, which had contained pigeon food, and holding a wooden spoon as though it were a weapon of protection. He was afterward to tell the boys that if he'd been one for the drink, he would have considered himself a victim of the DT's at the splendid apparition he now saw stepping from the car and advancing toward him.

"Can I help you?" he managed to say.

Sherbia, a respecter of persons however untidy they might look, bowed slightly and addressed him in very shaky English; he wanted to see the Brigadier Patricott. The name gave him some difficulty, though he was able to pronounce "Brigadier" recognizably.

Meanwhile, the boys, having seen the gaudy car glide past the house as they were giving their loft a vigorous scrubbing down, dashed up the drive after it and were rewarded by seeing the sheikh alight; as an Arab gentleman he was dressed in a dung-colored aba, on his head the white khuffiya with the distinctive square pattern in thin black lines, black headband, several strings of beads and a dagger tucked into his waistband. Nothing could have better rewarded their curiosity.

Joshua exclaimed, "Bejabers! It's Sherbia!" and James remained with his mouth hanging open, sighing a long "Cooooo!" He looked so amazingly out of context. A much lesser mortal, who had been sitting in the back of the car with the sheikh, now slid out and stood nearby, a bodyguard obviously. The "chauffeur" remained holding open the door, but turned and gave the boys a solemn-faced wink.

"Why, there's the brigadier's two sons themselves, sir," Mr. O'Duff pointed out. "They'll show you where their daddy lives!"

They greeted the sheikh with the Eastern dignity they had learned, then with great pleasure crowded in beside the chauffeur, who reversed the car and returned down the drive at their instructions. They had met the sheikh several times but had never lost their awe of him.

Everybody got out at the lodge, and Maggie tore fren-

47

ziedly out of the open front door, leaning over sideways like a motorcyclist going much too fast around a sharp corner. Slight dust flew up from her paws, so suddenly did she apply her brakes and give her whole body up to frantic high-pitched nerve-racking toy barking. It was as though all her life she had expected this sort of thing to happen; now it had happened and as she'd been saying all along. . . .

"What is it?" the sheikh asked nervously.

"Shut up, Maggie. . . ." The brigadier's shout brought a wonderful smile to the Arab gentleman's face, and the brigadier's appearance caused even greater pleasure. The sheikh embraced him, his hands on the brigadier's shoulders and his cheek pressed first to the left, then to the right cheek of his friend, a stream of delightful-sounding words pouring from him. Together the friends went into the sitting room, led by Maggie, satisfied now that the apparition had received endorsement from her boss. The mystic underprivileged one squatted down on the doorstep, his arms around his knees, and grinned up at the boys.

"A sheikh, eh? Friend of your dad?" the young man from Keele inquired, leaning nonchalantly against the Cadillac as though he owned it.

The friends talked; for nearly an hour they conversed in Arabic before the brigadier remembered that serving maids should appear with delicious honey wafers and tiny glasses of tea and became almost distraught in his anxiety to produce something similar but knowing perfectly well he could not do so.

He was trying to explain to the sheikh how it was impossible to fulfill his request to return with him to Janhara immediately to reason with the visitor's brother, who was in disagreement with the ruler regarding the terms of the sale of a newly found oilfield in the tribe's territory. This same brother was now rabblerousing, or rounding up Bedouin, the wild nomad brotherhood of the interior, against the ruler, because his idea of the terms of sale differed from those of the ruler. Once contented carpet makers, they had had the taste of money from their previous small oil finds and were as rabid for more as any industrialists in the Western world.

As the brigadier had been first British agent and then private adviser to the ruler, he was a trusted person, one who was familiar with the tribe's affairs and the only man to whom the ruler felt he could apply for personal assistance. He had told the new British agent this, and the agent had agreed that the brigadier's presence in Janhara immediately might be to good effect. The sheikh explained that there was no need to stay long; simply to appear among the Bedouin, many of whom knew him, would be effective, and an agreement might be reached which would certainly flatten his brother.

The British government was totally behind him, and it was at his request that Sir Francis Ansdell himself had asked the brigadier to fly out to the Trucial States. When the news that the brigadier might not consent to come had been telexed to the oil company, which at once communicated the news to the ruler in Janhara, he had immediately flown to Bahrein in his own plane and thence to London, arriving only this morning at Claridge's Hotel. He had to see the brigadier personally.

Excusing himself, Buzz went into the kitchen with Maggie at his heels, but started back to find Mrs. Flower still there. It was long past time for her to cycle home, but events had detained her.

"It's your shirts, sir . . . there are half a dozen to iron this week," was her excuse.

"Where are those bourbon biscuits, Mrs. Flower?"

She indicated the right tin and he snatched a half decanter out of the pantry, and with two glasses on a Woolworth tray he handed it to Mrs. Flower. "Please take them in to the Sheikh of Janhara; he is a ruler from the Persian Gulf." Though the sheikh would not drink port, the gesture would have been made without the shame of offering instant coffee.

Mrs. Flower glanced at herself in the mirror over the stove. She smoothed down her wispy hair.

"Go on, you'll do. . . ."

She curtsied, not low but a mere bob, for the occasion, and the sheikh took a biscuit from the tray without acknowledgment. She stood for a moment listening to the extraordinary speech, then retired. It was the event of a lifetime.

"I cannot leave my boys, Your Highness . . . I have put off my trip, I was coming, but I changed my mind . . ." Buzz tried to explain.

It was not good enough. The niceties had to be pushed out of the way. He had to bring up the squalid murder of a rich woman nearby and how he was involved. But it was wildly unrealistic, not the murder part, because it was very much on the old Persian rug that the Sheikh of Janhara might himself be murdered by his brother, but that he, the brigadier, should refuse to comply with the sheikh's desperate request simply because a woman who employed him, not even a lover, should have been murdered.

To Sherbia murder was a commonplace; what was unimaginable was that a *woman* should be murdered . . . that any man should be so incensed by a mere woman that he should murder her, seemed not to make sense at all. A tolerant man, however strict a Muslim, he barely concealed his contempt for the messy Western way of life.

But now having got down to raw truth, beneath the thick crust of compliment and superficialities, the sheikh resorted to bribery. Bribery is a horrid word under the British Crown, always followed by its mate: corruption. But not so among Arab gentlemen where it is simply a matter of business and common sense.

Extremely red in the face, the brigadier once more excused himself.

"Your Highness, I beg your leave to go to my room and think about this."

Upstairs he had his head in his hands, while Maggie sat beside him; it was impossible to see her face, but she sat rather than lay, out of deference to her master's turmoil of mind: she was on duty, as it were, and suffering with him.

What a fool he was making of himself! Why was it? He knew just what he could do to bring the ruler's brother to heel, to persuade him to come to terms with the proposed oil prices and to calm down the Bedouin. But he did not know what to do about leaving the boys, going to the police about tiresome dead Mrs. Furnish, telephoning his mother once again to say he had changed his mind about the trip to Janhara, telling Frank Ansdell that he was going after all, sending Maggie back to the kennels at once . . . why could he make instant decisions about some things sometimes and not other times? He held up his left hand as though blaming it for his indecision.

The door was slightly open, and Mrs. Flower crept in, ostensibly to put away in his wardrobe the shirts she had been ironing, now hanging from wire coat hangers; they were unaired, but the brigadier did not notice this or realize that Mrs. Flower was but making the shirts an excuse for entering his room.

"It's the sheikh who was one of my bosses, Mrs. Flower. He's in trouble back home, on the Persian Gulf. It was on this account the FO wanted me to go, and I've put it off owing to the mess about Mrs. Furnish; everything happens at once, doesn't it?"

"You don't have to go, surely?"

"No, I don't *have* to go. But. . . ."

She stood there, and looking up, he saw on her face such a look of kind concern that he said: "There's a great deal of money involved. I should be away, perhaps, three weeks and when I come back. . . ."

"Yes?"

"I should be quite . . . quite rich, Mrs. Flower. I could afford to send the boys to a boarding school; I'd have enough to pay a lump sum for both of them till the end of their school days."

Mrs. Flower nodded. "They should go."

"I know they should."

He had refused unhappy Mrs. Furnish's bribe of boarding school for the boys with no doubt whatever in his mind, because that would have meant Mrs. Furnish for life. . . . This meant a pleasant holiday in circumstances he enjoyed . . . and for three weeks.

"Is it in our old empire where you'd have to go?"

"No. Janhara was never in the empire. It is not really a country, but it was part of the oil territory where certain Bedouin were predominant. The sheikh was merely the

51

head of the—well, in a way—family. British influence in that part of the world was pretty strong since oil was struck, you see, Mrs. Flower. He's not really royalty as we know it—we call him 'Highness' from courtesy."

"I thought we'd done away with all that a long time ago."

"It looks as though some of them can't do without us, doesn't it? We've got a deep-rooted imperial instinct, but you wouldn't know what that means; we still feel slightly responsible for them—besides, there's all the oil! I was the British agent for some time, but when we packed up I was constantly called in as official adviser to the ruler. He wouldn't have needed any more advice from me, I would think, if it hadn't been for this new oil find. They are greedy over oil, you see, but who isn't? In the past when I have helped him, I've been given splendid presents, those rugs we have, the best up on the wall . . . all handmade and worth a great deal of money, but I could never sell them. This time, Mrs. Flower, this time he needs my help desperately. It's a matter of life and death."

Mrs. Flower looked distinctly startled. "Don't you get yourself shot, now!"

"Or stabbed, or poisoned, or strangled, or hanged. . . ."

"You're pulling my leg!"

But he wasn't, he was talking to himself.

"Look here"—Mrs. Flower was beginning to get excited—"I'll come and sleep here whilst you're away. I'll look after Maggie, too. Not to worry, everything will be all right this end. You go, lovey!"

The brigadier stood up and pulled down from the top of his wardrobe his soft camel-skin traveling case; there was not a speck of dust on it as there would have been on a case kept on top of the wardrobe belonging to anyone else. He opened it.

"'I'll pack for you," Mrs. Flower said, and started folding the newly ironed shirts.

He stood and watched her for a moment, then said: "I'm not happy about going . . . it's too weird that all this should happen just when our friend Mrs. Furnish was shot. It looks as though I'm getting out. . . ."

"Eh?" Mrs. Flower practically shouted. "What are you going on about? So what, she got herself shot; there's no knowing what that lady was up to on the Q.T. She was kind to you, so you're always saying, given you the job you like doing . . . it was only that she was an interfering b . . . lady. She thought she was doing good. Oh, I understood her perfectly. You and the boys . . . she thought you helpless, she was *helping you* . . . you don't shoot folk who is helping you." Mrs. Flower had been carefully packing while she talked, and now she picked up his shabby bedroom slippers. "Will you need these, sir?"

Though there seemed nothing to laugh at, he suddenly laughed. He opened a bottom drawer and brought out the heelless slippers he used to wear when on a visit to the tents. "These . . . the carpets they put down in the tents are so precious you can't walk on them in ordinary shoes; you approach the Presence in these kind of things. . . ."

"Well I never!" Mrs. Flower chuckled.

From the back of the wardrobe he brought the lightweight suit he had not worn for two years. "I hope I've not put on weight," he said, handing it to her to pack. "Mrs. Flower . . . you do me good." He looked at her puzzled. "You're so normal, somehow. Homemade bread and honey. . . ."

"What's that?"

"Oh, never mind . . . sorry. I can't take any of those shirts, Mrs. Flower. I'll take the thin poplin ones, terylene's no good in all that heat. . . ."

It had come to something, the brigadier thought, when you had to give high tea to the Sheikh of Janhara, but that is what it amounted to; maybe the sheikh did not think it at all funny that he should be fed by Mrs. Flower with eggs and tinned beans (bacon, of course, being out for a strict Muslim), which the boys enjoyed with him, while Buzz Patricott went to the police station to make his affidavit.

"What is an affidavit?" Joshua hissed into his brother's ear.

"A thing for keeping cats in," James said. But as that

was always the answer when he did not know the correct one, Joshua had to accept it.

The bodyguard had refused to partake of either eggs or beans and continued to sit upon the doorstep with his arms around his knees, something which the boys found entrancing, telling Mrs. Flower that the "slave lies across the bedroom door at night! He doesn't eat when he's keeping watch."

And after the meal the sheikh gave his whole attention to the television; being Saturday afternoon, there was no lack of fine entertainment. He was particularly fascinated by the cricket match in progress.

And then, while washing up, Mrs. Flower was nearly thrown into a panic by the arrival of Sir Frank Ansdell. He had been here before more than once, but for him to arrive when there were already visitors of an unusual kind and no preparations made was almost too much for her.

The short, stout man whom she served faithfully and with such pleasure had suddenly become a being apart and far above her; a gilded creature going about Her Majesty's business with other gilt-edged and important people. She was dizzy with it all.

In fact Sir Frank Ansdell's visit was now unnecessary, he had come to persuade Buzz Patricott to change his mind; he had received the telephone message turning down the job from the FO when he returned from golf at lunchtime and had come at once. There was no one available who could speak fluent Arabic and nobody anywhere on a Saturday who knew the exact position of that particular tiny state relating to the oil concessions. That some greasy adventurer should have struck oil in this particular small disheveled state (little more than a hamlet) at a time when everybody believed the oil wells to be drying up was of immense importance to the oilmen from various countries; the advantage the British had was that they knew the importance of being on excellent terms with the wild men of the desert. Thus Buzz Patricott had to be dug out of his greenhouse at all costs. On his journey Sir Frank had had many ideas, and one of them was so far-fetched as to suggest that Buzz take his two boys with him and dump them

54

for three weeks at the European school in Bahrein where they had been before.

All this was unnecessary as James, the elder son, rising to the occasion, told him. The sheikh being gummed to the television, James, with a great sense of responsibility, conducted himself with dignity. "We'll be perfectly all right, no need to worry!" He was straddling a kitchen stool, Sir Frank sitting on the edge of the kitchen table and Mrs. Flower doing the remains of the washing up and taking her time over it to listen in.

"The thing that put Father off going was Mrs. Furnish getting herself shot last night . . ." James explained fully. Was it really only last night? "He spent the evening with her, you see. Oh, it wasn't his fault, she was *after* Father, she was set on marrying him. . . ."

Joshua in the background did some realistic retching, by way of illustration.

"Well, of course, he didn't *want* to but he did like working in her greenhouses; he's potty about growing things. . . ."

"It's because he never has," Joshua put in. "All his life he's been in hot dry places, and he's never been able to do what he really wants, and that's what's made him so grumpy and strict and not liking children."

Sir Frank tried to hide his bewildered look in a large soft handkerchief with which he felt obliged to cover most of his face.

He folded it away finally and said that they seemed to have a grip of things.

"But don't worry," James comforted, "he'll be back soon from the police station, he's only going to sign an . . . an affydavid, he said so. . . ."

They embarrassed him, with their piping voices and their sophistication, they were like a couple of rather too clever stage children, he had never liked children on the stage. Peter Pan made him feel sick.

"Anyway, Mrs. Flower is coming to look after us, not our granny, thank goodness."

"Don't you like your granny?"

"Oh, yes! But she's so fussy, we've always got to be

washing ourselves, and she wouldn't like the pigeons we have. . . ."

"Had?"

"*Have*," James repeated firmly. "She'd say we'd *catch* something . . ." and Joshua did the illustrations, as it were, by scratching himself overrealistically.

"Well, I mean, you *can* catch something if you don't keep the loft clean!" James pointed out.

"Anyway," Joshua put in, "we're glad Father is going; we could easily have looked after ourselves, but I suppose everybody feels better now Mrs. Flower is staying all the time, so she says."

"Would you have liked to go with him?" Sir Frank was really curious to know.

"Not really," James answered for them both.

"We liked the school in Amman but the school in Beirut was too strict, and I got asthma from all the dust," Joshua explained.

". . . and it was too hot for us, really. Try playing football in the middle of the afternoon!"

"—on dried mud," Joshua added.

"Why are you glad your father is going?"

James scratched his ear and finally said cryptically that it was more like he was. When asked to explain, he blustered a little, saying, in effect, that his father had always been, kind of, important and now he wasn't, sort of. Just working in a greenhouse . . . and Joshua put in enthusiastically: "He was always dashing about the desert in a Land Rover nearly hidden by dust clouds, and now he stands poking about in a hot wet greenhouse all day being pestered by Mrs. Furnish."

The sheikh's dark, frigid presence in the hustle and rush of the sudden departure would have been intolerable had it not been that he appeared almost to have discovered television and to be watching it for the first time. This was not so, but the Saturday afternoon program was exactly what the ruler enjoyed. Mrs. Flower and the student from Keele University became very pally in the kitchen, and the bodyguard, though he refused to move from his position on the doorstep, was looked after by Mrs. Flower who failed to persuade him to have cups of tea and biscuits *ad lib*. Sir Frank sat in the brigadier's chair and put up his feet, closing his eyes and waiting patiently for the takeoff.

Because she went everywhere with him, the brigadier had Maggie tucked under his arm when he returned from the police station. "Well, I'm free to go," he announced. "They are adjourning the inquest for a fortnight, and then if possible for a further fortnight, so I will be back by then. They have to get the daughter over here anyway and haven't yet traced her. Now, Frank, I'm ready to go."

"Your boys have kept me amused."

Reminded of them, the brigadier went to look for them; they were putting the final touches to the cleaning out of their loft. Mr. O'Duff, it appeared, was giving them another hen pigeon to replace the shot one. This new one was still sitting on eggs and had to be left where she was in his loft for the moment.

"Well, now, look. . . ." The brigadier gave them short precise instructions as to their behavior during his absence. As a favor he asked them to take Maggie for a walk every day after tea, being sure to keep her on the lead until the common was reached; only then could they let her off but NOT TO LOSE THE LEAD, and if they did, CARRY HER BACK HOME. If they did not lose the lead, they were to be sure to put her on it before starting back home. "Tie it around your waist, one of you," was his final advice.

He carried Maggie upstairs and laid her upon his bed, saying very firmly: "Good-bye!" Maggie knew perfectly well what this meant. She settled down into the eiderdown; pressing her chin down into the comfort, she put her paws neatly in front of her to show she was cooperating. The hair, which always hid her face and showed only tiny shining slivers where her eyes were, seemed unaccountably to have parted, and out stared her disproportionately large, shining, slightly bulgy eyes. He turned away quickly and ran downstairs.

There was one more thing, and for this he wished to be alone.

The sheikh, the bodyguard and the young man from Keele went out to the car. Sir Frank went too and up the drive to turn his Mini. James and Mrs. Flower carried out suitcase, dispatch case and light raincoat, and Joshua fooled about with an umbrella, pretending it should go too.

The brigadier hurried back into the sitting room, stood upon a chair and felt about behind some books in the top row of his bookshelves. He brought out the small revolver in a plastic bag and another plastic baglet of bullets: he put them into his pocket and had only just replaced the chair when Joshua rushed in for him.

"All ready, Father. . . ."

"Coming, boy, coming. . . ."

Mrs. Flower was still absently holding the raincoat. "Will you need it?"

He took it from her and while he gave final instructions about Maggie's food, he slipped the revolver from his jacket pocket into the raincoat.

Overexcitement, perhaps, caused the brigadier to touch Mrs. Flower gently on the chin, raising her face a little. "Thank you, thank you . . ." he murmured, then, scarlet in the face, climbed into the Mini beside his boss and friend.

The gesture of his hand that the ruler gave as the equipage left the lodge was right royal.

7

"And now," Mr. O'Duff said, "tell me all about it. What's going on down there at the lodge, I ask meself. Nothing went on for twenty years whilst me old Mrs. Tring lived there, except that in the end she finally popped off." He giggled. "That was the only happening in all those years, believe me."

Mrs. Flower had sent the boys up to see their friend again, though it was midevening, while she bicycled the two miles to her home to make arrangements to spend three weeks at the lodge. The boys had to promise to be in bed by nine; she would try to be back shortly after.

They told him in turn and in fragments what they felt they knew, and he grumbled that the sheikh had not been brought up to the house to meet this son of ould Ireland. He had never met a Highness before, never. They discussed Sir Frank Ansdell, who had been so keen for their father to go back to the Persian Gulf with the ruler that he had come expressly to see this was done, and had left, following the Cadillac to the airport, and would probably stand upon the tarmac until the party had taken off. Their general disapproval of their father was for the present submerged in admiration and, it must be admitted, pride. Not many boys had a father who was needed so badly that he had to be fetched by a ruler of a country, however small and insignificant, to set right matters in that said country. James said that he was going to do foreign languages when he was old enough; he might even go to the college near Beirut to which his father went for the learning of Arabic.

There was a dreadful bantering manner about their friend O'Duff. Always good-tempered, he indulged in humorous ridicule, but he had great qualities which outweighed the boredom and embarrassment of his manner.

He sobered up when they returned to the subject of the double murders: the young bird and the old bird. "Now it's up to you two boys to straighten these troubles out." To talk in this sober manner as though they were responsible citizens was one of the qualities they so much appreciated. "There's not much connection between the two murders on the surface, mind. The bird and the lady bird, ha-ha! Folks are trigger-happy these days, the first thing a babe learns is to point a pistol at his mum and shout BANG! So it is not all that surprising that a bird was shot *here* on the same day as a grand lady bird was shot *there*, eight miles away. Tell me more about this Mrs. Furnish."

"She was just one of these kind of pests," James explained, "but not so's you'd shoot her, reely and truly."

"And what do you think, Joshua, me bhoy?"

"I'd of shot her if I'd of had a gun!"

"Come now, me wild man, I heard from all accounts she was very good to you."

"That was the trouble," James murmured.

Unaccountably Mr. O'Duff laughed till he choked, crying in gasps that they would be the death of him. He wiped his face at last, and, still coughing, said he understood that Joshua would have killed her on principle, in which case it might be considered an assassination rather than a murder. This fascinated them. Sitting at Mr. O'Duff's knee, as it were, they learned or thought they learned that murder and assassination were two entirely different things; you committed a murder for personal reasons and you assassinated for a principle, and when he was asked to explain what a *principle* meant Mr. O'Duff's face took on an almost saintly look, and he said simply and after a bit: "For others. Amen. Me brother Cart is a MAN of PRINCIPLE, now." He sat for a long time, smoking and staring thoughtfully ahead. Then he pressed out his cigarette stump with extra caution, as he always did, and said that now they would get down to business and he would tell them what he had in mind for them, first as compensation for the loss of their hen, *extra* compensation that was (since he had already given them another, verbally) and the second because their father had gone away for a time; it would keep them occupied when they weren't at school.

The cupboard at the bottom of the kitchen dresser he called the glory hole because it was almost jammed with a number of unused and discarded objects which he had not had the will to dispose of.

Living as he did in his kitchen and the servants' quarters adjoining, his numerous possessions became almost litter, and it took him some time to find anything. A confused din took place as he struggled to extract from the glory hole's internal muddle what he required.

They recognized it at once; it was a racing pigeon clock, albeit an old one, battered somewhat but very similar to the one Mr. O'Duff used himself.

"It's the one me dad had." Mr. O'Duff was breathless from the struggle and the amount of dust roused. "And I'm now going to donate it to me two young friends with many good wishes for some big successes!"

It was a marvelously complicated so-called clock in a

large, shabby leather case. When a pigeon fancier had entered his bird for a race, he took the clock along, set at the exact moment the bird had been thrown—that is, started—and these figures written on a small piece of paper would be inserted into a compartment at the side and locked in. The clock would go on ticking over until the bird's return, when the exact moment of its entering the home loft would be recorded and the number of miles and speed between the start and finish would be decoded in front of the judge or umpire and the winner discovered. Over this static and shabby so-called clock Mr. O'Duff's own father had spent many breathlessly exciting times.

The boys had often been shown the working of Mr. O'Duff's own smart clock, and they now examined the gift with exclamations of delight; to have one of their own was really something.

"Now I've a fine young male bird I've had in mind to give you for some time, since I have enough on me hands, in all conscience. So don't get the idea I'm being all that generous. I'm handing him over to you by and by to train as a first-class racing bird; you can enter as the owner of a racing pigeon for any race at any age, so it's all to be done in your own names, joint names, and I've entered you as members. Now as you well know, if I hand you a pigeon and you take it back down the drive, it will still come back to where it first saw the light of day when it broke out of its egg as a squeaker, you know that, now don't you? So what do I do? Leave it to the ould duffer!"

They were considerably interested to hear what, in fact, he proposed, since his own loft was on the sunny side behind the west-facing house and they were never allowed to go inside, though they could spend as much time as they liked above the stables, watching the pigeons strutting around in the wire-fronted "playground," as they called it.

Mr. O'Duff had this doubtfully comical way of postponing news, which amused nobody but himself. He made much of lighting another cigarette and taking a draft from his tankard of what he called porter, which was standing by, and then burst the news upon them that he had made them a barrel loft; he had been keeping it a secret from them and had taken the barrel away from the house, down the shrubbery walk into the old paddock; had they not seen it?

They had not; they never went into the paddock.

He had put the parents in there last mating season, and there it was, all ready for them, with one of the squeakers very nearly a racing bird all ready for training, mother and father living in the barrel alongside their son and plenty of room for flying around outside. He said he had always thought he kept his own loft too near the house, and had wondered whether it would not be a good idea to move the whole thing to the paddock which offered plenty of open space all round. It was a tryout, really, after that time, did they remember, when one of his homing racers killed himself on the new color-television aerial he had had put up last year.

He said that the fact of the matter was that he wanted to keep his valuable flock as near him as possible, but having them close to the house did mean they hadn't the freedom they would have in the paddock.

"There's so many thieves around," he went on, "it would worry me silly having them all down in the paddock. But there it is, I can't make up me mind to move the lot." All very circuitous but Mr. O'Duff's way.

It was dark now and the pigeons closed up for the night. The boys were exhausted, though they would not have admitted it, from their lack of sleep the previous night. They staggered down the drive, holding the heavy clock between them. Mrs. Flower had not returned, but they climbed into bed almost gratefully and were deeply asleep when she came, with her battered fiber case tied onto the back of her bicycle with a fraying piece of binding string.

She had put up a camp bed for herself in the tiny lumber room. The brigadier's mind had been occupied with subjects other than where Mrs. Flower was to sleep, but she chose the humble bed rather than the comfortable one plus a misunderstanding with Maggie. The brigadier's bed with the brigadier in it was one thing—the brigadier's bed without him in it—well, it still had to be treated with respect.

Mrs. Flower was slightly frightened of the boys; she did not understand them, they differed immeasurably from her own two children, though she could hardly have explained accurately in what way. If asked, she would no doubt in great travail have tried hard to respond: "Oh, in every way they're different; well, for one thing, they're far too grown-up for their ages, poor little things; I don't say they're bad boys, mind, but it's all due to their mum dying and they being left with their poor father, like; they talk too much, in my opinion, they're always talking, talking in ever such a grown-up way. . . ."

Mrs. Flower's offer to stay for three weeks in their father's absence was due entirely to her wish to help and support the brigadier. She shocked herself at her own readiness to do something which she did not really want to do, but having said she would do it, she intended to do it to the best of her ability, and a Sunday morning was always a good time to set forth with new resolutions.

Determined to keep the meal conversational, Mrs. Flower sat with them around the breakfast table, a model group which could well be an advertisement for a crackling corny breakfast food.

"Well, we didn't half have some excitement yesterday, eh? I've never known anything like it in my life, I haven't."

She smiled kindly as she stirred her tea. "A murder and a sheek, and a dash off to foreign parts at a few minutes' notice, affidavits and statements and the lot, and all in one day, eh?"

"And our hen pigeon shot the day before, don't forget," Joshua said with his mouth full.

"I do hope you'll be specially good boys," Mrs. Flower said hopefully, "and you get your homework done, James lovey."

"We've got more important things than homework to do," Joshua said darkly. "We've got to look after our new hen pigeon that Duffer has given us, and train the new racing pigeon that lives in a barrel in his paddock. . . ."

"And find out who killed Mrs. Furnish, so the police don't bother Father when he comes back. . . ."

"And that, too," Joshua echoed uncertainly.

"And find out who shot our hen pigeon."

"Well, you've got a lot on your hands," Mrs. Flower said comfortably. "Are you sorry you couldn't go with your father on this trip? It sounds a lot more exciting than anything you could be doing here."

"Exciting!" James exclaimed. "It's not exciting in the Middle East, we were born there, Mrs. Flower, and there was never anything *exciting*, was there, Joshua?"

"Well, the sheek was exciting, you must admit," Mrs. Flower argued.

"We often saw sheikhs," Joshua grunted disagreeably, "but we were surprised to see him here, he looked funny, didn't he, in the drizzle, I mean?"

James, having finished his breakfast, tilted his chair backward in a way which always annoyed his father. "Two days ago I was thinking what a pity Mrs. Furnish lives so near! Today I am thinking what a pity she lived so far. Becos . . . becos . . . what we ought to do is go and water Father's plants in her greenhouse; who is there to do it? I bet the bobbies won't."

"That's very nice of you to think of it, James," Mrs. Flower said, and after a moment's thought added that perhaps their friend Mr. O'Duff would take them over, to oblige. He had a motorcycle and a Merc. And besides, he seemed to have plenty of time on his hands, not an old man by any means and he seemed to have retired! she marveled. "What does he do with himself all day long, anyway?"

What did he? "He looks after his pigeons," Joshua suggested.

But not all day.

"He'll be reading the *News of the World* now," Joshua mused, "and then he'll go out and feed his birds and then. . . ."

". . . start getting his dinner ready . . . frying."

Mrs. Flower said that for sure cleaning the house wouldn't be among the things he was going to do. She'd never understood what for he wanted that great house with all the windows shuttered and all the paint peeling. And look at the garden! Weeds so high, right up to some of the windows!

However active the boys' minds might be, this was one thing upon which they had never speculated. They accepted it as they accepted other eccentricities on the part of people around them, such as why their father should choose to spend his day in a steamy greenhouse picking tiny seedlings out of the boxes with special pincers. Speculations about the unorthodox movements of their elders seldom bore fruit.

James wiped his mouth on the back of his hand and suggested they go at once to ask him why he lived alone in a big shuttered house, but he only wanted an excuse to go.

Mrs. Flower was flowering, she thought of herself as climbing into their world, she was making great efforts to please. She went on to say: and what was all the traffic that passed, she wondered, up the drive to the house?

"Traffic?" How unobservant they perhaps were, after all.

"Well, not big lorries, of course, but vans pass up and down, every day. I'd say there was one at least, sometimes three or four, in a morning. Haven't you noticed?"

They shook their heads vaguely.

"That's why Brigadier had the fence put around the lodge, he was having it done the very day I came, a new fence and the gate to stop Maggie going out into the drive. *What*? I thought, what's the traffic up the drive about? I thought, and I'm still thinking it."

They stared at Mrs. Flower in her new role of thinking reed.

Joshua folded his arms and moved cozily, sliding up the bench to be nearer Mrs. Flower. "What do *you* think the vans going up and down the drive are about, Mrs. Flower?"

"Well"—Mrs. Flower smiled with pleasure that she was attracting some notice—"well, I can only guess, can't I?"

They agreed she could only guess.

"I have a new guess every time I see one pass."

"What sort of thing do you guess, then, Mrs. Flower?"

Mrs. Flower sat with her chin in her hand, inadvertently in the same position as Rodin's Thinker. "Well, it could be something good or something bad. . . ."

"Oxfam," James suggested, trying to hide the smile at his own brilliance.

Mrs. Flower shrieked with laughter.

"Is that good or . . . bad?" Joshua frowned.

"It's good, of course. But since I've been here there's been ever so much traffic, I mean for a private house, it couldn't hardly be goods for Oxfam, could it? No, I'd think it more like to be battery hens. . . ."

"You have to have a shed for them, and anyway we'd know if it was battery hens, we couldn't help but know."

"It could be he's keeping it secret; there's people against battery hens, like antivivisectionists, they could come along and wreck the place one night, maybe. So he keeps it secret, keeping them in the house more likely! Racing pigeons ain't a bad cover for the battery business. He's a kind sort of chap, from what I know of him, which isn't much, I admit."

The boys sat silent and wondering.

Mrs. Flower was going from strength to strength: "And that Mrs. Furnish, I shouldn't wonder she was in it too!" She was enjoying herself thoroughly in her effort to engage the boys' attention. Thoughts, even words, which she had not known she had ever had, now crowded into her head, and when she said: "I often wondered," it was not true; it was simply that she had had a thought which she now remembered she once had, and this started a train of subsequent thoughts which she was almost inventing as she went along.

Almost but not quite.

There are thoughts and *thoughts*. One kind of thought you sit and think for hours, days or weeks, and there's another kind of thought which whizzes through your mind almost unnoticed, so that later you may bring it up from the subconscious and call it a thought for want of a better name.

"There was that old Mrs. Tring who lived here for years and years, ever since Mr. O'Duff came here; in fact, she was here long before, she was cook to the people once owned the house. She died a couple of years ago, I know because she was a member of the WI, and though she'd given it up for quite a time, at a meeting they mentioned that she'd passed on, I remember it clearly. How did your father find this house?"

"We were looking for a place to live," James said. "We were living with our granny in London and Father was at his club until we found somewhere in the country to live, and Father sent to house agents for details of houses in the part he wanted to live, not too far from London. A little house, we wanted, and to rent."

"But don't you remember, James?" Joshua put in. "We had lunch in a hotel after we'd seen that horrid house with the beastly smell. . . ."

"Yes, I remember," James shouted, "and you flung out your arm like this and sent your Coke flying, and in a scramble to pick up the glass Maggie came out from under the table and there was this woman sitting at the next table and she said"—and James imitated her with hideous precision—"'Oh, what a marvelous little dog, so ti . . . ny, wee . . .y.'"

"That was the beginning of it," Joshua remembered. "She and Father got very chummy, and then we all went into the lounge for coffee and Father told her we wanted somewhere to live. . . ."

"And she said she knew just the place, 'tiny but cheap,' that's what she called it . . . and to let . . . not for sale. Just what Father wanted!"

Joshua leaned back against the wall and blew out a lot of air: "So we've always known her, seems like. . . ."

"Well, after you've done your homework and attended to your pigeons, the new ones, too, you'd better start doing some detective work," Mrs. Flower suggested whimsically.

"But how can we? We can't exactly get into her house even to water Father's 'precious' seedlings as he calls them, let alone playing detectives."

"So you can't." Mrs. Flower started to clear away, she had done so well that she felt it a setback not to be able to solve that one. The pickup was still standing outside under the rhododendrons which dripped in the drive.

"Tell you what"—they perked up instantly—"our George will be at home from London soon, and be along to see his mum for sure; he'll take you over there in your dad's pickup; your dad did say the pickup could go for a maintenance whilst he was away, come to think of it, but we could keep it by us for a bit anyway, and ask the garage to take it when Brigadier's nearly back home. He said nothing to me about his seedlings, but he'll be pleased we've remembered them, anyway."

Mrs. Flower went upstairs to "do" the bedrooms; the boys went into the living room and shut the door. Joshua pulled an upright chair toward the bookshelves; it was the same chair that the brigadier had pulled up to the bookshelves a moment or so before his departure. James spread out the contents of his satchel as though he were doing his homework.

Joshua stretched up and felt about behind the books at the top of the bookcase.

"Don't bother, it will have gone," James prophesied. "It's so small, but I knew the old man had it in his raincoat pocket . . . because why take his raincoat anyway? I could have laughed. . . ." He made a small dry spit into the air.

"Die? I thought I'd laugh!" Joshua brought out a small box which had contained cartridges but was now empty. "There were a dozen and there's a spare box here!" He held it up.

"He's taken them loose in his pocket, those he didn't fire at his girlfriend . . ." James said bitterly. "He looked like a dear old gent going off for a holiday in the sun, but I saw the droopy weight in his mack pocket; it weighed about a pound unloaded, he told me once."

Joshua sneezed.

"Nobody ever dusts up here, it's a good place to keep a gun."

Breathing heavily, he climbed down, and sitting astride the chair, he asked his brother what they were going to do about it; what did they really intend, was in his mind, but he was unable to ask it in so many words.

Were they looking for something which would prove that their father shot his friend Mrs. Furnish? Or what? It was time to elucidate their intentions or, as Mrs. Flower would have put it: What were they playing at?

James was now lying straight out in the big armchair, his hands clasped over his nonexistent stomach. "We want our freedom, don't we?"

"Of course . . ." Joshua agreed uncertainly. "Freedom to what?"

James frowned. "We've had all this out before. Freedom to do what we want, of course."

Joshua squatted down with a fearsomé frown upon his face. "But we *do* what we want."

"We certainly do not!"

"Well, there's certain things we don't want to do, like take LSD and smoke pot."

"Yes, we're weaklings in that way, but there's two of us so we can do things *we want* to do, cos we're two. We don't *have* to do what the others want to do; if we did . . . it wouldn't be freedom, would it?"

Joshua's face did not straighten out at his brother's lucid explanations, it took on another expression, non-comprehension. "I don't smoke it cos I'm frightened," he said, and after a pause added: "What is freedom?"

James sighed heavily. "Oh, you're just a stupid kid!" He was seriously annoyed, since his brother was asking the very question to which he, James, himself wanted some conclusive answer. But after a time during which a listener would have believed he could actually hear the machinery of his mind turning over, he said: "I seem to know better what it isn't than what it is. Like . . . well, you're not free if you're locked up. And you're not free if you're not allowed to take drugs, and you're not free if you can't take things out of shops without paying."

"But those are things you can't do anyway."

"Who says?"

"Well, you *can't*. . . ."

James felt he was making a hash of explaining freedom. "It's a mistake to start thinking," he hedged, "you get all muddled up."

Joshua tried to help; he changed his position and expression. "Well, what does FREEDOM FOR WOMEN mean?"

He screwed up one eye and looked at his brother with the other with a look which said: Well, solve that one, you clever dick. He had seen it on posters in a London procession on the TV.

"I don't know the details"— James pursed up his lips like any judge—"and I wouldn't like to mislead you. . . ."

Joshua cupped his ear as though straining to hear: ". . . to what me?"

"Mislead!" James shouted.

"Do you know what I think?"

"No idea, how could I?"

"Father could have shot Mrs. Furnish because he wanted his freedom."

James did not agree; he shook his head thoughtfully. "What would be the good of that, he *liked* working in her greenhouse, he *wanted* to, it would be just plain daft if he shot her."

"He shot her because she was such a nuisance and I think he won't come back home, he"— Joshua waved his hand vaguely—"he'll disappear . . . is what I guess!"

8

Mr. O'Duff's brother came and went, and at every visit there seemed to be a different car parked in the stable yard near the back door. Up to a point Mr. O'Duff resembled his brother, who was of a more sober version altogether.

At first they were incredulous about his name, Cart, until the Duffer explained to them that it was in fact a Christian name, such as James, but not, he was sorry to say, Joshua, which was pre-Christian: "One of these Old Testament blokes," he said contemptuously. But Cart was named after a saint who died on May 14, which was his birthday. Furthermore, this St. Carthage died at Lismore in Ireland, just a few miles from where the vast O'Duff family originated. What was fascinating about Cart was that he had been a monk, a full-blown real-life monk for thirty years.

He had left home at fourteen and joined a holy brotherhood, much to the pride and delight of his parents, at that time immigrants to England, running a garage. Fortunately these two sainted folk had died before the awful event of Cart leaving the brotherhood had taken place; it would have broken their hearts that Cart should have gone back on his vows.

"But, mind you," Mr. O'Duff pointed out warningly, "far better to get the hell out of it than eat your heart out leading a life you've definitely finished with in spirit. I think it was brave of him, brave and wise, and anyway fourteen is far too young to decide to give your life to God, and that's me candid opinion, so help me God!" And he crossed himself for luck and forgiveness for his opinions.

"So what's he doing now?" Joshua had asked in his irritating pipe.

Mr. O'Duff made great play with his hands. "This and that," he explained, "this and that! Oh, he's the bhoy, he's doing fine things . . . fine things. I'll tell you this, he's the one in our family of ten kids that'll write his name in the book!"

"What book?" Joshua wondered.

"The book of life, bhoy," Mr. O'Duff failed to explain.

They were a bit, hardly frightened, but awed by Cart, whom they could hardly fail to meet on their frequent visits to the big house. There was no regularity about his visits; he might come twice a week, and then they would not see him for many weeks. When they asked Mr. O'Duff how it was that he had so many different cars, he laughed and said he hired them. Since he lived in Ireland and came over to England very often, it was cheaper to hire.

But he, too, had an interest in the Fancy and he and Mr. O'Duff would spend hours standing in the big loft, discuss-

71

ing the birds. He was kindly to the boys but paid them as little attention as would have been paid to himself as one of a family of ten.

If Mr. O'Duff could be said to love anything, it was his birds; he would pick them out and hold their beaks against his face with the utmost tenderness; he would hold them toward the boys, expecting them to feel the beaks against their cheeks; it was as though he wished to share with them the intense pleasure these lovely pigeons gave him.

And it must be said that he did indeed wish to share his hobby in the same mood in which he might expect his own sons to follow in his wake. Intimations of mortality and lack of a son, or child of his own, may well have caused him instinctively to try to pass on his own addiction, and it might not be too far-fetched to believe that he felt that if he were to die suddenly, as people do, there would be someone at hand, ready to attend to his lovelies.

In a glass case against the side wall of his loft were the trophies he had won in a lifetime of pigeon racing; the boys had been carefully shown the first, which he won at the age of eighteen, and the last one, which he had gained the previous year.

"And now James here is going to follow in my footsteps," he explained cheerfully to his brother. "And listen here now, Jimmy. . . ."

There followed many explanations and details about the time and place of the first big race of the season, and finally they all, including brother Cart, went out to the barrel loft the Duffer had given them. It was a hundred yards or so from the house, and though it would have been visible from the end of the yard in winter, there was now a thick screen of foliage on the fruit trees which had remained long unattended but which produced usually much fruit in due season, all of which fell to waste, no village boys now could be bothered with ripe Belle de Louvain plums and Cox's orange pippins.

"You see, they're screened here from the yard and there's nobody to overlook . . ." Mr. O'Duff had explained to his brother Cart.

"But would it matter, Mr. O'Duff, I mean, if anyone did see us?"

There was a slight pause. "Of course it would matter; you don't want the whole world and his wife to know what you're at, now, do you?"

Joshua supposed not.

They stood around admiring Mr. O'Duff's handiwork: an old "porter" barrel precariously fixed at the top of a washing-line post, the marvel being the perches Mr. O'Duff had managed to fix inside. He described it proudly as a "furnished residence."

"It's going to be a surprise to the world when a boy of twelve wins the next county race. 'I was a cradle champion!' you can tell the reporter who calls on you on your hundredth birthday . . . you've a sport of a lifetime here, you won't have to give it up at forty with heart trouble. . . . Isn't that right, Cart? Football, boxing, tennis, even cricket, there's an end to it long before you're old. . . ."

"Not to billiards," Joshua said, and Mr. O'Duff cuffed him lightly on the ear.

"But what's all the blood?" Joshua squinted up at him.

Mr. O'Duff did not look at him; he kneeled on one knee to struggle with a shoelace while he tried to unravel the question. Cart, who had been only half listening, swung around. "What does he mean—*all the blood?*"

Trying to help his brother over a moment of embarrassment, James explained pigeon racing was a blood sport, of course, didn't he know that?

"I see." Joshua frowned, uncomprehendingly. "But you said you'd given us a hard-bitten couple of birds with blood you never cared for, but we'd do fine with them. And you've just said, up there in the loft, you've done fine with your blood importations, you said that too."

Mr. O'Duff felt his leg was being pulled. "Run off home, you monkeys, I've had enough of ye. . . ." He looked red and ruffled. "And run away down across the paddock and go over the gate and up through the field and through the rhododendrons to your lodge; that way you don't pass the house and I don't have to see you every day!"

"Do you think he's getting sick of us?" Joshua asked as they walked out of earshot.

"He's getting sick of you, I should think. Were you fooling?"

Joshua denied it indignantly. "I don't know what he's going on about half the time," he said, aggrieved.

"He didn't like you talking about blood. . . ."

"Why not?"

"Well, some people don't. It makes some people pass out. Besides, he didn't mean that kind of blood."

"Well, what sort of blood did he mean?"

James said nothing; he climbed over the gate from the paddock into the adjoining field. He did not know the answer.

"Well?" Joshua repeated.

"I don't know everything," James snapped.

As they were pushing their way through the rhododendrons, Joshua wondered out loud why Mr. O'Duff was so kind to them.

"I'll tell you what," James returned confidentially, "he's not so nice when Cart is there, is he? I mean to say."

"He's ashamed of knowing us when Cart's there. But I think he does really like us because if not, why go to the bother of making that barrel loft? I say, do you think it's a bit wobbly? It might fall down on us one day and kill us."

"It's not heavy enough to kill us."

"He was kind to give us the racing clock, but will we be able to use it?"

"He said he would show us how to work it and repair it and oil it, but he won't when Cart's there, will he?"

"Oh, it'll be all right, I daresay. We must try not to annoy him! Do you like Cart?"

"No. Do you?"

"No."

Back in the dismal kitchen at the big house, Mr. O'Duff brought a packet of bacon out of the larder and tore off several thick strips, flipping them into the frying pan he already had on the gas stove.

"I want none," he said. "I'm feeling none too well."

"You don't look it, Con brother, you don't look it," Cart remarked.

"I could do to be more ruthless in me ould age, like you, Cart."

"Ruthless, me?" he screeched.

"Yes, ruthless, Cart."

"There's yourself, getting soggy, as you say, in your ould age."

"All of forty-four," Mr. O'Duff said bitterly. "And I have me moral obligations!" His unsettled eyes glanced uneasily about him.

"You have indeed! You're a member of the Republican movement in both political and military wings, and so am I, and let's hope neither of us forgets that, sworn over our dying father," his brother reproved.

"Yes, over our dying father, it was for sure."

The bacon was sizzling energetically, and from his armchair Mr. O'Duff was able to open the kitchen drawer and bring out a carving fork, which he now waved menacingly at his brother Cart. "I have neither the desire nor the inclination to. . . ."

"One and the same things. . . ."

He forged on: ". . . inclination to cause fires or explosions!"

Cart opened his mouth and made a lengthy wordless noise which could be described as a medium-sized roar.

Mr. O'Duff got up and prodded the bacon, turning over one piece which was burning. "Not here, where I now stand. It is not the policy of the movement we belong to, to engage in such acts in Britain."

Cart was restless; his brother Con became tiresome and argumentative sometimes, he had had this kind of thing happen before. It must have been that child talking about blood that had upset him. For an assassin his nerves were much too taut.

"Don't be too nice about it, too particular. Fire, arson . . . and you-know-what . . . it's all part of the conspiracy."

"I did not conspire to kill. . . ."

"What does it matter? If you hadn't killed, as you call it, your brother members of the organization would have

75

been arrested, good and proper, they would. Either you're wholeheartedly a member of an organization, or you're not. Make your mind up; don't turn milksop when the plans go a bit wrong."

"You know I'm in it heart and soul, and I make no apology to anyone for it; I'm an Irishman every living cell of me and a Republican all me life. I shot that damned nosy parker of a woman the same way a soldier in wartime shoots a guerrilla he sees pointing a gun at . . . at *someone* else! That's just the way it was and I'm no more guilty than that."

"Well, what's wrong wid you, then?"

Mr. O'Duff smote two eggs upon the side of the frying pan; they joined the bacon, and there was an enticing smell, but still his face bore a look of distaste.

"I'm fond of those two kids, can't help it, maybe it's because I've none of me own. I made a mistake not marrying and having kids, too busy thinking about revolution, and one revolution in particular. Kids keep you young. And you've had no kids yourself, Cart. We've missed out both of us."

"Don't you be too sure I've had no kids."

Mr. O'Duff's face became very wry; he hid the lower part with his hand as he so often did when he was trying to hide a smile from the boys. He said: "Well, I've had no time for philandering with women. I've been too busy with birds in me spare time. . . ."

"You've had plenty of time learning how to make bombs and incendiaries and passing your knowledge on to others. . . ."

Mr. O'Duff deftly switched the bacon and the eggs onto a plate as one who has done it many times and at the same time demonstrating how dexterous he could be. He banged the plate down in front of his brother and cut him a thick slice of white bread. He pushed the butter toward him and sat down again at the table, watching him eat, with distaste.

"So I see you're really off your oats!" Cart observed.

"I'm worried, I'm really worried, those kids suspect their pa shot the old nosy parker as you call her, and I'm not sure they're the only people think the brigadier did her in."

"Oh, come off it!" Cart begged, his mouth stuffed.

"It's not so mad, she's been running around after him ever since they came here, nearly two years ago. It was she told them the lodge was to let in the first place; she's a magistrate and knows everything. They'd been out to dinner together, and they went back to her place after. I can guess they had some sort of blowup. She was a tiresome sort of female. I've seen her in court, and when her husband was alive, they'd call at the garridge for petrol, times. There was always a bit of fuss, always something not quite right, like. Yes, a real tiresome old bag but generous, mind. She offered the soldier man a job in her hothouse, and did he leap at it! Seems hothouse flowers was a lifetime's hobby."

He cut his brother another piece of bread and finally decided to have one himself. He got up and put the kettle on, laid two cups and saucers, fetched milk, found sugar.

"Cut it out," Cart said curtly, "you're having second thoughts about something that was unavoidable, absolutely an act of duty that could not be avoided. She asked for it; what right had she to come up here and snoop around to the extent she did, on somebody else's property, and when you were out?"

Mr. O'Duff sighed heavily. "I was only popped up to the loft for a coupla minutes and left the door open." He nodded toward the back door. "I'd got too slack, that was it, after all these ten years I've felt safe. I do me shopping, I go to me pigeon meetings, I lead a pretty normal life in this dead-alive hole; me visitors tell me when they're to be expected. I'm practically the country gent. I've welcomed the presence of those boys and even their soldier father. Old Ma Tring couldn't even get herself up the drive, let alone snoop . . . I caught this new intruder at it, red-handed as they say!"

Satisfactorily fed, Cart leaned back and stirred his tea; he let his brother go on, he felt it would do him good. In fact he encouraged him: "Go on, Con. . . ."

"Well, these here moral obligations . . . she had plenty of time to look at the labels in the one room she managed to get into—the butler's pantry; oh, yes, she was all there! It would be where I'd dumped a consignment of machine guns with their spare ribbons and all—just till I'd decided where I'd put them . . . temporary. . . .

"The quicker, the better, thought I, she can't live with all that guilty knowledge, she mustn't be given time to pass any of it on. But I had to wait till dark and long after. The midnight break-in and robbery was the thing. I've heard a lot about her from those two boys, they hated her guts, they thought she intended to marry their father, and they grumbled to me something awful. She was lonely or something, they said, and she was longing for a new husband and ready-made kids and all this and all that. So it might seem she was all alone all night in that blooming great house, like I am here, come to think of it. And what do you think? Starting off for the Red House, I went down the drive here on the motorcycle and there was the Rolls parked here at the lodge! Beat that. Right, I thought, I'll hide in the bushes or wherever along at the Red House, and when she gets back home I'll come up behind her and fire as she gets out of the car, no need to go into the house and leave fingerprints all over the place, glove prints I mean.

"But blow me! When I got there, at the Red House, parked the cycle down by the gates, hidden in some bushes, what do I find? Lights on in drawing room, hall, and elsewhere; didn't actually see milady. So what did I do?"

The telling of the story was doing him good, his eyes brightened and his manner cheered up considerably, he was almost boasting now.

"I rang the front-door bell. She wasn't afraid or shouted who's that or anything like that; she'd never been molested before, that's for sure. The door was on the chain, though; she opened it, looked through four or five inches space, and I said would she very kindly let me in, I wanted to talk to her about what she had found this afternoon at my house, very polite. She said there was nothing to say and I said oh, yes, there was, I said, since I'd caught her red-handed; I said it was only fair she should hear my side of the story. First, she'd no right to explore my house and second, I was a dedicated man, I said, and had been all my life . . . I was an Irishman, I said, and I had moral obligations to the Republican movement, I said. Dammit, man, I made a speech! And what do you think she said, had the nerve to say?"

He couldn't guess.

"Well, since it was her turn to talk she let me in first, then she said: 'Oh, you're one of those, are you? It was *me* caught *you* red-handed, my man!' "

"My man! I'd have knocked her down!" Cart exclaimed angrily.

"*You* would, I didn't. She calmed down and actually asked me if I'd like a tot of anything to drink and I said very earnestly . . . no, I'm teetotal. I apologized at coming at such a late hour, I said I'd not intended to come but I had come, just in case she had not retired for the night, *retired*, mark you. It was because of me moral obligations. She told me to sit down and I squatted on this round thing on the floor and she sat down on this awful high-backed fancy kind of settee with ropes and dingle-dangles and she was pulling down her skirt not to show too much leg when I whipped it out, and holding it at arm's length, I fired. I wasn't a foot from the target: left breast or heart? No, I decided on the head, since she's a stout woman and the bullet would have less work to do!"

"What did you use?"

"That little Browning automatic, thirteen shot magazine . . . on the way back I threw it in the river!"

Cart roared with laughter; he slapped his thigh and laughed loud and long. "You threw it in the river!" He mopped his face, weeping with laughter.

But Mr. O'Duff was deathly sober.

"She turned out a decent old bird, asking me in, and all. I would never have done it, never, *never* have done it, if it hadn't been for me moral obligations!" He refilled Cart's cup with thick dark-orange tea: "Do you know what is wrong with us, Cart? We're idealists gone bad . . . gone sour . . . gone stinking rotten!"

9

Joshua went up to his father's room and picked Maggie off the bed. She growled gently but that merely meant "Hello!" Because there was nobody to observe, Joshua kissed her between the eyes, or where he guessed her eyes were. He had often done this when there was no one about; there was a secret relationship between himself and Maggie. To appear to be fond of Maggie would be soppy and might presuppose a good relationship with his father. He held her tiny body close to his own and told her to cheer up. He whispered: "Rats and mices . . ." and Maggie leaped from his arms and made a dive for the back of the wardrobe, where she pressed her nose to the tiny space between it and the wall and blew impressively; Joshua flung himself on the floor and made similar loud sniffs, gradually working Maggie into a frenzy of excitement so that her tiny tail moved so quickly that it vanished like the spokes of a bicycle when rotating sufficiently fast. As her whimper of excitement grew in crescendo, Joshua rushed around the wardrobe and snatched her up before there came a wild high barking. "Now come on down to lunch," he whispered, "and if you sit under my chair I'll give you something worthwhile."

Mrs. Flower had a secret one-and-sixpenny (old currency) manual called *How to be a Lady* and one of the tenets she had underlined with her red ball-point was: "The upper classes converse as they eat at meals." Though there were many things of which she did not approve (such as "total immersion in hot water is necessary every twenty-four hours"), she certainly approved of conversing at meals. As a widow she was entitled to her daydreams and one of the most far-fetched was that one day she might marry the brigadier; she was attracted by short, stout men and it did no harm at all to learn a few of the principles of correct behavior in the vague hope of attracting the only one she knew. But manners apart, she evinced a kindly interest in the boys' activities.

Thus it was that Mrs. Flower gradually became aware of their belief that their father was a murderer. And what was worse, their calm acceptance of it. If "boggling" be a verb, it must be said that her mind boggled quite considerably. "They can't really believe that!" she told herself many times, and when finally she gave up trying to accept the evidence of her ears, she tried to "have it out with them."

"You don't really mean that, James! Why do you keep making these, as you call it, snide remarks? It's not true, of course, but it doesn't *sound* nice. It's a very, very nasty idea when you and I know quite well that your dear father wouldn't hurt a fly. I don't know. . . ."

"You don't know what, Mrs. Flower?" Joshua asked with seeming concern.

"I don't know where you get your ideas from, really I don't!"

"Maggie wasn't there; she was still in the kennels." Joshua was holding Maggie on his knee, putting tiny scraps off his plate into her mouth. "He'd never have done it in front of her."

It was that remark that relieved slightly Mrs. Flower's mind. They were playing at believing, that was all; their minds fed on a diet of murder and mayhem in picture form, they carried on the pretense. Thank heaven for the pigeons, Mrs. Flower thought; they must be encouraged vigorously.

Thus she threw herself wholeheartedly into the pigeon game, constantly asked after the squeakers that were being patiently and faithfully watched over by the lone pigeon widower and duly rejoiced when they flew. When her son came home for the weekend, she had him down to the lodge and got him to repair the racing clock. He was very interested in this, and he and the boys spent a whole day studying it and practicing the use of it, once it was in working order.

But then Mrs. Flower became gradually aware that James believed their father had gone never to return and this frightened her, too. James was a more stable child than Joshua, he had a sense of responsibility beyond his years; at times when Joshua was at his most volatile, James was at his most stolid. When Joshua became most optimistic and forward-looking about their pigeon-racing successes to come, James became his most sober and sensible, pointing out their lack of experience.

"But Mr. O'Duff says so!" was Joshua's constant cry, and James and Mrs. Flower would exchange the understanding smile of the elderly.

"Mr. O'Duff is a very nice man," Mrs. Flower pointed out, "but it would not do to take everything he said as gospel."

"How do you mean?"

"Well, I only know him to say good morning to when he passes here on that motorcycle of his and slows down to make a pleasant remark. But I'd say he's typically Irish, and they're an airy-fairy lot."

"Leprechauns and things," James explained helpfully.

"That's right, James." Mrs. Flower found James saying just the things she would have said if she could.

"All the time he seems to be teasing," James went on; "he doesn't answer a question at all! Haven't you noticed, Josh?"

Joshua wasn't going to criticize his idol; he made a face.

James went on: "I asked him why he lived in this lovely big house and kept it all in the dark with the shutters closed and all the doors locked, and he snapped at me: How did I know the doors was locked? I said I tried them, at least two of the downstairs ones . . . and he said I was a naughty boy, there was leprechauns in them rooms and he only let them out at night, they slept all day, he said." James giggled, showing how absurd such a concept was to a boy of his age.

Joshua's face wore a wary look. He had heard this and half believed it in that it appealed to him; he wanted to believe that he was in a houseful of sleeping leprechauns, but knew it would be shaming and babyish even to pretend he believed it. Only a baby would believe in something he could not *see!*

But thinking of leprechauns and that most unleprechaunlike character Mr. O'Duff's brother, he said now openly that he didn't like Cart because "He's cross inside; Con is laughing inside, that's the difference."

Then they excitedly told Mrs. Flower the plan Mr. O'Duff had for their racing a pigeon in a race later in the summer; that it did not matter at what age they entered and they joined in on an equal chance with people who had raced all their lives. The clock had been explained to her, and now they divulged that Mr. O'Duff was racing a pigeon next week and he had asked them to keep a watch for the pigeon's return. It was coming from the north of England about three hundred miles, they said, and Mr. O'Duff would be on duty at the clubroom in the town, checking on the whole race. So they would have to stay around his loft and watch and watch for the homing bird, and it might all depend on the wind how long it took.

"I don't know *why* they come back . . ." Joshua piped.

"Nor does anybody!" James said sternly. "It's in-sting."

"And sometimes they race all night, on and on in the dark, miles and miles . . . a thousand miles. . . ."

"We've got to wait for Mr. O'Duff's bird to come home, and *then*, when it arrives, we've got to take off the ring they put on its leg when it is thrown, with the starting time on, and drop it through the slot in the clock, see, Mrs. Flower?"

"And then you turn a handle so's you can't get the ring out anyhow, no one can but the man who has the key and he's at the pigeon club, so you take the clock there next day and they open it and find out how long the bird's taken, see, Mrs. Flower?"

"Well, I never!"

Mrs. Flower felt a certain pride that things were going well in the brigadier's absence; she felt tempted to write him a little note to tell him so; if she addressed it to him at the Foreign Office, she guessed it might arrive, but she refrained from actually doing so because she thought superstitiously that it might change their luck. Better to keep quiet and hope for the best while, perhaps, fearing the worst. The boys had never been intractable, but Mrs. Flower had to accept the sad truth that when their father was there, they were more sulky, well, she could not even say *more* sulky because they were not at all sulky with her alone.

Joshua, for instance, appeared to take no notice of his father's dog when he was there; their whole manner was one of indifference, but alone with them, Mrs. Flower found them as young and enthusiastic as any other normal boys. She spent much time when they were away at school turning over these thoughts.

She thought things would be different when he came back; she had had a breakthrough with the boys, and she felt she was now in a position to help. Something would have to happen, she felt, and it must be on the way to happening, since no family life could jog contentedly along if the children believed their father a murderer. Even to put her thoughts into words embarrassed Mrs. Flower; she was not one to wander in the realms of fantasy. Still, she did wish very much indeed that they could hear something about how the inquiries into Mrs. Furnish's death were going, if they were going at all. She made a point of going on her bicycle to the supermarket every weekday morning when the boys were at school and dallying about in the hope of meeting people she knew.

She did in fact meet many acquaintances, but found that they were perfectly prepared to stand and gossip about this and that for minutes at a time without any reference to the murder at the Red House. Eight miles was a long way away; the television brought Tel Aviv right there onto your lounge hearthrug, so that yesterday's murder there was more real to you than the murder eight miles away; and what with today's murder, not to mention tomorrow's . . . last week's and eight miles away and a magistrate at that! It was nearly forgotten.

Thus every journey back to the lodge on her bicycle depressed Mrs. Flower; you could die and nobody really cared; you could drop out of the world, disappear into nothing any time, and nothing would be different; would the people she talked to in the supermarket even mention it to one another? Mum's dead, her children would say, but so what? Poor old Mrs. Furnish, all that money and that car!

That lovely house and the greenhouse! And what about the daughter in America? She couldn't even bother to fly over to see what was what, it would seem.

Mrs. Flower was so overcome with her own weighty thoughts that she wandered to the brigadier's room and picked Maggie off the bed, holding her tightly and murmuring: "You and I would care very much if our Buzz was killed . . ." and she blushed with pleasure because she had at last actually said his name out loud.

And thus a fortnight slipped past in harmony at the little lodge with its carpeted walls and its two baby pigeons with their father doing double-double time over the feeding and the boys giving him all the help and encouragement they had time for after school.

They were more interested in the little family on their doorstep than in the young pigeon couple living in the barrel in the paddock. They dashed up with food in the morning and evening, but they did it as more of a task than they undertook their care of the home birds.

Joshua brought things to a head by saying unexpectedly: "Bags, you go up to the barrel; I'll do ours out. . . ."

James was washing out the meal bucket; he carefully turned off the tap against the yard wall and looked searchingly at his brother.

"No, I'm not getting sick of the blood sport . . ." Joshua exclaimed quickly. "But I. . . ."

"But you . . . what?"

"To tell you the truth. . . ."

James's heart jumped a little as people's do when they think you really are going to tell them the truth. Anticipation of it is often better than the realization. "Go on then!"

"I think there's . . . some . . . thing . . . phony . . . about . . . it."

"About what?"

"About him going to all that trouble to make that barrel for us, I mean, it must have taken hours, and keeping it a secret from us and all that. Where did he do it? We would have seen. And. . . ."

"Um?"

Joshua's brow was deeply furrowed but not with the trouble of expressing himself; he had no difficulty in doing that. It was his own thoughts which puzzled him.

It was an important enough subject to sit down over . . . they sat down, their backs against the back of their loft.

James confessed that he had had thoughts about that kind of thing, too. "He's kind, he's terribly kind to us, but not *that* kind, I mean, spending hours making a barrel loft and fixing it up in the paddock and the stepladder up to it and all that. It's like he's gone too far!"

"Shouldn't wonder if he bought it secondhand from a friend. . . . I've looked very, very carefully and it seems to me that floor's been scraped before, and for pigeons," he hissed.

James was impressed. Joshua was in so many ways an infant, yet in equally many ways Joshua had more brains than he; his mind dodged about here and there, as James thought of it, in the maddest way, but often he perceived truths of the matter a long time before his brother. However, he said that he, too, had had a feeling that there was something *going on.*

"And *I* don't think Father shot our pigeon," he added; he had wanted to say that for a long time.

Joshua narrowed his eyes in a sinister manner but did not subscribe to that opinion. After a long time he said that the Duffer was under the influence of his brother. "Haven't you noticed how different he is to us when he's there? Oh, he doesn't think he is, but he seems to be putting it on: 'We're jolly good friends, the boys and I.' It makes me. . . ." He was lost for an adjective to describe what it made him.

"And me," James readily added.

"I have the sort of feeling," Joshua muttered so that James had to lean forward to hear what he was saying, "I have that funny sort of feeling that he has got a bit sick of us." Joshua made an awful face, squinting up at the sun and distorting his features considerably. "I mean . . . the way he told us which way to go back home when Cart was there the other day. . . ." He waved his arm, demonstrating.

"Doesn't he want us to pass his house anymore?" He added importantly and very much in the brigadier's manner, "I ask myself."

After another long pause James remarked that Joshua had said that before. "We were going to do some investigating about Father and Mrs. Furnish . . . we didn't get very far."

"I got bored with it," Joshua said in disgust. "It was so obvious. Not that I'm blaming Father; it was assassination. I'd have done it myself if I'd had a gun. . . ."

Now he had gone out into the wilds, as he so often did. James said scornfully: "You had a gun, Father's. You could have shot Mrs. F. yourself, but you just didn't think of it!"

"I did."

"You didn't!"

"I did!"

"You didn't!"

"I tell you *I did!* I did, I did!" Joshua screamed.

James folded his arms and let it lie.

"But will you look after our new pigeon couple, while I investigate?"

"No, I won't," James returned at once. "I'll investigate too."

"It makes sense to . . . to divide it . . . we haven't much time; if we both investigate and both feed our new couple that takes double the time than if we did it my way. And there's your homework, don't forget."

This was the unconsciously insolent remark of the bright child; Joshua did his homework in a flash, often incorrectly, but James had to plod slowly and painstakingly to achieve his results which were usually better than those of his brother.

After another long period for thought, Joshua went on that what he meant was: Look at all the things they'd seen in the television news! Look at all the bothers in Ulster and guerrilla warfare and all that. . . . "And look how the Duffer sits about talking about ould Ireland and all that. Well, do you know what, 'me bhoy'? He's a member of the Irish Republican Army. He boasts about it."

"Well, so what? He can't do any harm . . . he never goes to Ireland, that we know of!"

"We haven't known him all that long, he's maybe been to Ireland a lot, he only hasn't been away since we've known him, and that's not two years yet."

James murmured pacifically that it was only when his brother was there that he talked Irish; when they were alone, he was a fine companion, they talked mostly about pigeons; look at all they had learned from him! In James' opinion, he only wanted to show off to his brother. "Look at Cart's clothes and his shoes and the hired cars he comes in. He's the one who made good while old Duffer sits around all day in his kitchen, except when he's looking after his birds."

"He goes out a lot in the evening and at the weekends. . . ."

"He goes to see his pigeon friends and the club . . . they're never at home during the day. He *often* goes out at night and I've *often* heard him coming back, sometimes on that old motorcycle of his, and sometimes I've heard him creeping back awful late in the Mercedes."

It should have been more exciting that he was the owner of a Mercedes, but it was of such age and respectability that it had long ceased to have any glamor.

"But, Josh . . . wouldn't it be really marvelous if he did . . . I mean . . . the *first time* . . . we can't really do it on our own."

"You mean . . . race the new pair . . . I mean, one of them, *this summer?*"

"If we could just do it, with him sort of, this once, then next time we could do it alone . . . next time and every time after. . . ."

"So?" Joshua asked coldly.

"So whatever he's done or not done, or even if he is getting sick of us, let's keep him at it till we've *really raced,* just once!"

88

10

The criticism they had for their benefactor would seem unjustified in view of the trouble he took over their training as fanciers. Indeed, he was starting them on a lifelong hobby and gratuitously instilling in them all the right principles, meeting halfway any inward-turning tendencies these preadolescent boys might have. To say that he was doing them the good turn of a lifetime would not be overstating it; why, then, should there have been any criticism, anything other than complete loyalty?

Yet an observant adult would instantly be aware of something in Mr. O'Duff's manner that was vaguely repellent; a tenuous and evanescent quality, a manner perfectly described by Scott: "A doubtful, uncertain sort of twilight rationality" which met and mingled so uneasily with his haranguing about Ireland and himself as an Irishman.

The plans for the first big race of the season had been made. Mr. O'Duff's female bird was in what he called "fine snuff"; it was her second season, and during her first season she had flown in many training flights of gradually increasing distances. The wind being chilly and due north, the weather was fine and dry, and the distance, he reckoned, would easily be covered from the starting point to home, in a day. On the Friday the basket containing the beautiful blue-white racer was collected in a truck picking up other contestants.

"She will be back home tomorrow before dark with this fine strong wind behind her," Mr. O'Duff said. "Now then, when you've had your tea this next day you two boys will come up here and you and I will go to the pigeon racers' club in town, James. You're the eldest and you're doing the admin, so it's right I should take you and not Joshua, but Josh has an important job; he'll have to stand by his post like a sentry and never far away *no matter what.*"

Joshua reddened at the great weight of responsibility that seemed to have fallen upon him.

"Don't worry, me bhoy; there's a telephone in the loft and you can ring your Mrs. What's-it down at the lodge if anything goes wrong. But there's nothing will go wrong. You'll suddenly see me bonny blue-white girl flying in . . . oh, bhoy! the thrill of it. You open the trap, you know how, Josh, and in she goes and you'll slide this ring off her foot and slip it in the clock, which I'll leave just here, so don't move it."

There was a shabby canvas deck chair in the loft and a packing case upturned serving as a table. "This is where I always sit and read me paper. I'll leave you some sandwiches and a bottle of water. Now don't worry if it starts to go dark . . . I believe she'll be here in record time with this fine wind blowing her south, but there might be some mishap at the other end, the sort you know, where there might be some fool mucks it up. And James and I will be at the club and we'll be back betimes. I may telephone to see if me beauty is home, if we're delayed."

Far from feeling elated, Joshua was depressed; there were so many small things he could think of that might go wrong. The trapdoor . . . he tried it once or twice and it worked perfectly, but Joshua knew that it might stick just the once, the first and last time in a lifetime, when he was looking after it. If the bird delayed going in, precious time ticked away and was lost.

"You're thinking the trapdoor will stick, eh, Josh? It won't; I examine it carefully every race. But what will drive you mad will be the bird might dally, that's what I call it . . . dally. They're all in a rush to get home and yet. . . ."

"Yet what?" James asked steadily.

"And yet . . . they can mess about, just mess about . . . looking to see if there's a bit of grub . . . oh, anything. As I've often remarked when I've heard others grumbling about how they lost the race by seconds because their pretty Polly just wouldn't go straight in, stood nearby first on one leg, then on the other . . . but as I always say, they're only human, after all, and you can't expect them to behave

90

like machines. They're not the Concorde." He sniggered at his own joke. "They have their little weaknesses like us all!"

At teatime Joshua was filled with a sober self-importance, and James wistfully wished he had not to attend the office job with Mr. O'Duff; he would much rather wait with Josh to see the racing bird swoop down out of the sky. It was surely more exciting than mere monitoring as the clocks were brought in.

Mrs. Flower asked if they would be home after dark and James said he thought so. He would be coming home with Mr. O'Duff from the town in the Merc and they would go up to the house to see if the pigeon was safely home. "And Josh and I'll come straight back after that, promise . . ." he said.

Mrs. Flower said that in that case she would go and see old Mrs. Somebody, her great-aunt in an old folks' home, whom she had not visited for some time. "But I'll be here when you come back, for sure."

"You won't be there if I ring up, then," Joshua grumbled.

"You won't have to ring up, Josh; nothing can go wrong; what are you afraid of?" James asked.

"I've never done it before." Joshua opened his big eyes very wide and put a sorrowful expression upon his face: "It's a big important thing for a little boy to do . . ." Both Mrs. Flower and James burst out laughing, as Joshua had no doubt intended.

Nevertheless, Joshua did have that left-out feeling when the Duffer and James climbed into the old red Mercedes, and it must have shown on his face because the Duffer leaned out of his window and said in his husky, confidential voice: "You're doing a great job of work, me bhoy. But then your brother is going to be useful, too. I've got to introdoos him to my buddies at the club, mind. We're all for the younger generation, us up there, they're going to have to take over from us when we get too long in the tooth to fill the food buckets, to mix a metaphor. And some of us is wondering where the young men is going to come from to take over, see?"

Just as he was moving off Joshua rushed after him. "Mr. O'Duff, Mr. O'Duff. . . ."

He stopped: "What is it, mannie?"

"What's the difference between a pigeon and a dove?"

"None at all, none at all, but what you have to remember is . . . a pigeon's a pigeon and a dove's a dove . . ." and with a sly glance and a wave of his hand he drove off.

Joshua went back into the loft. He sat down in the deckchair and picked up his book: *Pigeon Post*. He read avidly for an hour, then picked up the elderly but excellent binoculars, took them down into the yard and holding them up to his eyes, scanned the horizon. Would it come in quickly and mysteriously like the great airliners slipped in at Bahrein airport? There would be no speck in the clear, Middle Eastern, ever-blue sky, then suddenly the monster plane would be just over there, hedgehopping the airport buildings quite silently, with the noise trailing along behind in an immense roar and seeming to fly away overhead on its own while the plane landed.

It had not been a completely clear day, but now the sky was clearing as it often did before sunset. He longed for the bird to come; he very much wanted to be reassured that it was really coming. To him it seemed a miracle that it should this morning early have been released at a place somewhere north of Glasgow and that it should appear here, in Mr. O'Duff's yard, at any minute. He was certain it was not going to happen. And he was ready to cry with disappointment. He worked himself up into a slightly hysterical state so that he was trembling inside. The awful responsibility that had fallen upon him grew in proportion to his anxiety. It was all wrong and a mistake on Mr. O'Duff's part to have left him alone in the loft and to have taken James to the club in town; it should have been the other way around. He felt aggrieved now, as well as apprehensive, and when a large bird flew over the loft and landed on the stone pediment along the edge of the roof, he was certain it was the returned pigeon.

In the fading light it sat on the edge, looking down at him. Why, why did it not come straight to the loft, as Mr. O'Duff had sworn it would, even if it did not instantly go

92

inside through the trap which Joshua should be holding open for it? How could Joshua do his job until the bird was where it should be? In anguish he wrung his hands, twisting them together and biting his knuckles in extreme anxiety when he could no longer see it.

Something had gone terribly wrong. Joshua moaned.

The light seemed to be going rather fast now. Joshua looked wildly around him. There was a line of three windows behind the balustrade, only less than half of them visible from ground level. The top part of one of them seemed, from the yard, to show a small pane of glass missing in the leaded lights of one window. Suppose the ass of a pigeon had gone in there instead of coming to its own loft door?

Mr. O'Duff would passionately argue the point against a pigeon being an ass, but how could one be sure of its movements? If it had flown at seventy miles an hour for hundreds of miles, it might be pretty bewildered. The more he thought about it, the more convinced Joshua became. You can work yourself up into any belief whatever when you are entirely alone and feel yourself deserted in your hour of need.

Of course, Joshua knew the front door and in fact the whole house was locked up; they had often wondered why it was so important to keep an empty house so secure, but there are people, in fact the police encourage them, who are fanatics about locking up. Joshua, however, knew that Mr. O'Duff had a spare key in case he ever forgot to take his keys with him; he was not supposed to know it was there; it was hidden under a plant pot in his untidy potting shed leaning against the yard wall. He had snatched it up within seconds of thinking about it, unlocked the back door, fled along the stone passage, through the baize door cutting off the servants' quarters, into the empty stone-flagged hall, past the wide steps to the cellar under the stairs and up the shallow staircase; then the mean, narrow one leading to the servants' bedrooms.

He had never been up here before, but birds certainly had made full use of the top landing and passage, and they had flown in through a skylight which was partially broken, the glass lying on the floor below, together with evidence of rain, causing that part of the floor to be in a rotting state. Though Joshua did not know it, the house was air-conditioned so that it should always retain an even temperature; it was evidence of extreme carelessness on the part of the owner that the skylight should not have been immediately repaired, since the smallest intake of fresh air can cause big irregularities in temperature.

Joshua was daunted for the moment; beyond the little square skylight-lit landing the passage ran to a leaded window at the end, similar to the other windows as partially seen from outside. The passage was fairly dark, but not dark enough to hide the galvanized hasp passing over a staple and padlocked on each of the five doors. Fastened on the first door was a thermometer, and as he ran down to the window at the end Joshua noticed another thermometer on the last door. There was not the slightest hope of getting into any of the rooms, he realized at once.

He stopped thinking about the pigeon for a moment, so impressed was he by the exciting thought that Mr. O'Duff must be a robber, storing some infinitely precious goods, pictures maybe. Perhaps he was an international fence . . . or something.

Pausing, he stared with narrowed eyes at the leaded window at the end of the passage; he could easily, very easily, kick that in. He could climb out onto the edge of the roof, protected by the balustrade; then he could probably walk carefully around the edge of the roof to the window into which the pigeon had disappeared. Kick away a few more lights, and he might even climb in and rescue the valuable bird, *vivat vivat Joshua*! He was inclined to dizziness and in the ordinary way wouldn't have gone out onto a second-floor roof if he had been dared to, but this particular roof might well have been constructed for adventurous boys, protected as it was by the sturdy balustrade with its shapely (Queen Anne, though he did not know it) pillars.

Right.

He climbed onto the windowsill and holding onto the architrave around the nearest door, which meant leaning forward farther than was comfortable, he kicked backward hard, and with his heel broke one light, broke another; then

94

two more went, and looking behind to see the extent of the damage, he realized he could crawl through this now relatively glass-free aperture, feet and legs first, pressing the lead aside, in places tearing it.

Mr. O'Duff was going to be raving mad, he thought, as he wriggled out backward, but his anger would be assuaged by relief that his bird had been rescued; it would have been trapped in the attic, and nobody would know, or would have known, if it hadn't been for Joshua, the brave, enterprising young. . . .

"Hell!" The drop was farther down than he had reckoned upon and for the moment the breath was knocked out of him, but he recovered quickly and, taking his bearings, he advanced, face toward the roof because he did not wish to look down, protected though he was by the balustrade, in the direction of the broken window toward which he was aiming.

Here it was, with the broken pane in the top corner, and, alas, he had nothing but his bare fist with which to break enough panes to get inside. And the space was too narrow to allow for the successful backward kick he had just used to good effect. Oh, glory! What was Mr. O'Duff going to do if he broke all those panes all to no purpose? Would he beat him? He had often said that if either of them did so-and-so he'd "thrash them within an inch of their lives," and this they had always thought to be a kind of Irish joke. For a moment he wondered whether or not it might be a real threat.

He was wearing his school shoes; he grew out of them so fast that he had only one pair which he always wore unless he wore sandals, and the year was not yet far enough advanced for that. They were pretty heavy; since he had spent most of his life in sandals, it had been impressed upon him that in England heavy shoes were preferable. He took them off now, they were no good whatever for climbing, anyway, and stood in his thick knee-length gray socks bought him by an earnest father anxious to take the shop assistant's advice and buy "the right thing."

With all his weight, and that was not much, behind him, he crashed his shoes against the pane next to the broken one through which he was sure the pigeon had struggled. It broke, and the lead, even, was slightly bent. He cupped his eyes with his hands and peered inside, but it was too dark to see. He broke two more, then bent the soft lead, almost like Plasticine it was so old and malleable, he thought, into a space as big as the one he had just passed through, which was not very big. What a lot of damage he was doing in a very short time, he thought with satisfaction. He expected to hear a wild excited fluttering of the pigeon such as he often heard in the loft boxes. There was dead silence. Away from the walls but almost filling the room was a symmetrical square about four feet high, covered with a green tarpaulin in newish condition. He lifted the edge of this at once and saw a medium-sized tea chest with stenciled marks on the side, a letter or two, a few numbers, evidently to be understood by someone other than Joshua. He walked around, lifting the tarpaulin here and there, seeing the same tea chests, piled one on top of the other carefully, forming the tiny rectangle, three half-sized tea chests high, each of them with a rope handle at the sides.

Mystery.

And no bird of any kind, let alone a racing pigeon.

Not only was he shaking inside now, but his legs were shaking, too. He felt rotten, tired and sick, there was so little air in the attic room. He sat down with his back to the wall and thought what a miserable fool he was making of himself. "That's you all over!" James would taunt him.

The depressing thing was . . . it was all right boldly to carry out the plan that had sprung into his head at the sight of the bird on the roof; the trouble was it had now to be put into reverse. And the further trouble was that he couldn't just slip back to the pigeon loft leaving everything as it was, he had to go through the whole process in reverse, leaving obvious evidence of his mistake. Such pain and fear as he might have endured in the excitement of the chase vanished completely when it had to be done as a retreat from glory.

And now, did he or did he not hear a car entering the yard?

He did. And the others were back long before expected and would be looking for him, and he would have to get himself into a more dignified condition before he could face them, or they found him, fearfully crouching in forbidden territory.

However, the speed at which "they" came up the stairs and into the attic was frightening; he had left the back door wide open which would have shown anybody at once that he had broken, as it were, into the house. He shouted for help. They raced up the stairs as though in pursuit; they undid the padlock with some noise; they flung open the door and switched on the light.

It was too shaming and ghastly a moment to be supported; Joshua gasped out loud with sheer misery. Unfortunately it was not Mr. O'Duff; it was that awful brother of his who came and who went without any warning of his comings or goings, if, indeed, he had any reason at all.

It would be difficult to say which of the two, staring at one another in the cruel light of the central bulb, was the more shocked.

11

Mr. O'Duff rocked himself gently to and fro, as though at a wake, lamenting with a heavy breathing that amounted to a slight moaning commensurate with the situation.

Since it now seems that everybody's roots are so firmly planted in childhood that it is not possible to throw off that which one took in, as it were, with the mother's milk, what was the good of trying to do so? From the time he could walk Mr. O'Duff had looked up to his younger brother Carthage as a being only second to God. Even when, as a renegade, Cart had left the monastery, it was, somehow, a saintly act, done for others. He was freeing himself from the peace and holy quiet of the monastery in order to devote his life to the Cause. Others before him had been fanatics who took the Sinn Fein oath with all its phony bloodthirstiness and demonization, swearing to *embark for and take England, root out every vestige of the Accursed blood and the Heretics, Adulterers and Murderers of Henry VIII* in three hundred and seventeen words.

Since the great schism in the party, recruits now sign a declaration of fidelity to the party's aims, which is, when the verbiage has been stripped away, a simple one of eight words: *to Get the British Out of Occupied Ireland.*

Mr. O'Duff himself, in the abandoned fervor of the moment, had indeed signed the Awful Oath in the presence of his gentle, yet hard-eyed father at the age of eighteen and believed himself steadfastly to have adhered to it, though he was inclined to refer to himself as a "sleeping partner" with more humor than was intended.

But his loyalties were unfortunately divided because so much of the valuable time he could have given to the Cause went in looking after his pigeons; still, in fairness to his brother, Cart showed interest in his hobby because, in fact, "sleeping partner" or not, Con did what he was asked to do satisfactorily, very well indeed in fact.

Except that he had his soggy, sentimental moments . . . like now.

"It's not that you're killing the child," Cart pointed out reasonably. "No one could accuse you of an inhumanity of that kind, not at all, not at all . . . you're killing 'for the Blessed Virgin . . . by her sorrowing and sufferings at the foot of the Cross, by her tears and wailings.' "

"Ach! If I'm killing him for all that . . . why don't *you* do it?"

Cart's face took on an extraordinary expression; he did not so much roll his eyes as let them float upward till they almost disappeared up into the region beneath his eyebrows.

Mr. O'Duff observed him without emotion. "Well?" He waited for the answer.

"For three-quarters of my life I've lived in a monastery, and during that time I have learned to love my fellow beings; yes, I love them"—he held his arms wide—"I love everybody, I love them like Christ loves them."

It was a quarter past 3 A.M. and things said at that time of day-night can sound fairly reasonable.

Mr. O'Duff, however, was unconvinced; he continued to moan faintly and to rock gently.

His brother was impatient. "I don't know what you're going on about, Con. You didn't have any hesitation in taking out your gun and riding over there on your motor-cycle and shooting that woman who'd discovered about the arsenal you have here within, what, eight hours of her finding it? That was a neat piece of work, if she hadn't already reported her findings to the police!"

"I didn't give her time!" he snapped out of the side of his mouth.

"Ach! She'd plenty of time after leaving here."

"She went to the station to pick up her boyfriend to have an evening out with him . . . would it not occur to you that I followed her to see where she went? . . . You don't trust me and that's the sober truth!"

"How can I trust you? You could have shot that stripling upstairs in the attic several hours ago when you found him; you could have left him there in his sleep and no one would ever know a thing about it. Young boys are constantly disappearing from their homes these days; the police have so many on their books they can't hardly follow them all up. Sometimes when there's a shortage of news they make a thing of 'search for missing schoolboy,' but more often than not after a local look-round, the family keep quiet about it . . . little Johnny is off on the drug jag someplace, better the neighbors shouldn't know!"

"Ye haven't given me a reason why ye don't do this small deed yourself!" Con declared reasonably enough.

"But I have, I have . . . it's not for me to do it since he's in my care at present . . . inside I'm still a servant of God. . . ."

"Well, so am I! I do the dirty work, the dangerous stuff . . . I'm the brains behind it and all the energy, too."

He found Cart's words untrue and agonizingly hurtful. His gray little mouth twisted with pain, and he ran his bony hands over his exhausted face, miraculously keeping his temper. "Look, Cart, would ye go now! And by the way, what did you come for in the first place?"

"It's about the arrangements, May fourteenth is the day." Cart looked pleased and excited, as though this were an achievement over which they might rejoice. "And don't forget it," he added.

"Forget it? St. Carthage's death day . . . your birthday . . . as if I could! How are the arrangements going?"

"We have our troubles, and that's the truth. Mainly transport; it's the bona fides bother me; every delivery van has to be a sight so familiar and boring nobody looks twice. Oh, we're doing it all right, it's been done before, but in the meantime since last time there've been dropouts for various reasons, and it's just a matter of getting reliable drivers lined up. I'm all right my end, it's your end I'm worried about; this sickly sentiment because you couldn't raise your hand against a 'little child.' Really, Con, to put it mildly, you make me sick! Assassination is assassination, and if it's a blue-eyed baby girl or a nice boy, well, so what? Sentiment!" He spat slightly into the coke bucket. "Where are yer ideals, man?"

But Mr. O'Duff now wrapped himself into the kind of black, impenetrable mood that the Mountains of Mourne sometimes wrapped themselves into, and as he glowered up from under his eyebrows at his brother, it did look as though Cart might be leaving. Next, Cart went down to the cellar and brought up two full mugs from the barrel of their favorite drink made from Liffey Water of Dublin. He also got out some bread, butter and cheese and prepared a snack for himself; finally, he sat down at the table, bit a huge lump out of the white bread and cheese sandwich and looked across speculatively at his sulking brother.

"Are you wishing me to go?" he asked mildly.

"That I am," Mr. O'Duff snarled.

"I'll stay till you've done it . . . then when I'm gone, you'll be able to sleep with a *aisy* mind."

There was never a greater sophistry; Mr. O'Duff ignored it.

"Consider the practical side," Cart continued as though to himself. "Since that youngster got in, he'll get out, make no mistake. And the first thing he'll do is make off to the po-olice, seeing himself a savior of mankind. He won't know the word 'arsenal' . . . ammunition store, he'll call it. Won't they pat his shoulder and call him 'Sonny,' won't he be the little hero! You'll be inside for life, and as for me . . . it may take a little longer, but I'll be inside too, and for life!

"Right, you threw away your pet gun last week, but you've hundreds more, hundreds. Have you got one handy, Con, without opening a fresh case?"

Con was not going to discuss it; he said neither yes nor no; he said nothing. Cart finished eating, he drained his mug of porter, he made a display of tidying crumbs off the tabletop with one hand into a waiting hand below; he almost threw his mug into the sink, put away bread, butter and cheese, wiped his hand over his mouth and looked again speculatively at his brother. Con worried him, he knew all about this streak of sickly sentiment, but on the whole it had not interfered too badly with their activities. Now he saw danger ahead. The Patricott child was not harmless; far from it, he was a walking fuse—a bright-eyed intelligent child. However much he might be in Mr. O'Duff's thrall, the child would not be able to resist the exciting knowledge which he now possessed when he woke up. After all, his father was a soldier, and some of the soldier's way of thinking would certainly have brushed off onto him.

Uneasy though he was, and he was sick with anxiety, he was not going to allow himself to panic; if he panicked, he would do something silly, like shoot the sleeping child himself, and it would deeply grieve him to do anything dirty, because shooting an innocent child was dirty and would prejudice his chances in the Final Count. He was trained for many years to keep his soul immaculate, and free from taint of original sin it must be kept. On his knees by the table he sandwiched his prayers by two paternosters, rose to his feet and made the sign of the cross over his brother.

"God keep you, Con, and that is my last word. I've to be in Liverpool by nine, so farewell, brother. . . ."

Mr. O'Duff heard the back door slam after him.

It might be thought that anyone who collected firearms to the extent that Mr. O'Duff did might slake their fascination fairly quickly. But not so Mr. O'Duff; he was nothing if not contrary and the opposite to what one would expect. He went into his bedroom and shuffled back with another of his treasures, a neat "combat masterpiece" revolver with a six-shot cylinder. He sat down in his chair again with it lying flat on his palm. He had had an idea.

As Cart had been talking, the idea which had come to him had been so excellent that he now knew it had been the answer to Cart's final prayer and blessing. He was told, as from heaven, what to do with the small boy's body. One of the boxes piled in the master bedroom containing the gas-operated semiautomatic carbine was just the right size to take . . . a child's cadaver (cadaver sounded so much better than the common word, "body"). He would empty one of them, finding somewhere to store the contents, wrap the cadaver in one of those large plastic bags you could buy everywhere, and stow it inside, refastening the metal tape to look untouched. It could then be dispatched with all the other ammunition on the Great Day (May 14) and would not see light of day again until it was opened at the secret place on the wild mosses in County Kerry. And there it wouldn't matter; it would be dug into the earth in two shakes of a lamb's tail.

In the meantime, he was unable now to go upstairs and shoot Joshua before he woke, so that it would all be painless and civilized, and this was where he felt ashamed of himself; it was like giving way to drink or drugs. He would have either to wake Joshua now or wait until he had slept out his sleep in the warm dry attic, to ask him what in the name of God had happened to his racing pigeon. He decided to wait.

102

12

Buzz Patricott sat in the chilly airport lounge at Beirut and sipped thoughtfully at his large glass of fresh lemonade. The air conditioning was giving him a slightly stiff neck. It was a fortnight since he had left home. The stay in Janhara had been agreed upon as to take three weeks, but there was nothing more he could do there. He had written a long and explicit report which was in his dispatch case ready to take to the Foreign Office.

Though he would never say so, the job could have been done in a weekend; what he could never persuade people was that the Arabs "only need understanding" and by that he meant that they need, too, to understand. Communication was what had been missing in their discussions with the oilmen, who failed to understand that they were not talking business with one man, the ruler, but between two Bedouin factions of undying antipathy, whose initial quarrel went back into the dark backward and abysm of time, and what it was about probably none of them could remember. It was quite likely to have started with the mysterious death of a sheep.

The sheikh's brother could make threatening noises and promise instant revolution, but as soon as Buzz Patricott had him talking his own language almost to himself in his desert stronghold, sitting cross-legged at a low table, eating buckwheat garnished with an occasional sheep's eye, the problem dissolved. Exquisite manners, recognition of the other fellow's status and innumerable compliments were essential.

And not to hurry was another thing.

It mattered not at all that one could say the same thing over and over again; in fact, the more often, the better. Complete agreement was reached and Buzz drove back across the desert in a bouncing Land Rover to report to the ruler, bearing yet another exquisite handmade rug, vegetable dyes of pink and darker pink, marigold and azure.

The capital of Janhara had had no surprises other than concrete ones. The last time he had seen it, not so very long ago, it had been a village of mud huts, date gardens and waving palm fronds. Last time he was there he had slept in the back of a Land Rover wrapped in an aba; this time he stayed in the new hotel, no doubt temporarily whimsically named the Nasser Hotel, built of matchbox-shaped concrete rooms overlooking the tiny mosque. The din had been frightful, concrete mixers grinding away constantly. It had always been noisy, and he wondered vaguely what the noise three years ago had been. Street cries, iron-clad wheels, weird Arab singing, like a lament—all this was now probably still going on, but indistinguishable in the overriding modern sounds of building. Though there were excellent taps in his bathroom, four of them, no water ran from them; they were ornamental.

Sherbia had been restless to see him and to hear how his visit to the interior had gone; finally the ruler carried him off to his country residence, a small pavilion built of marble blocks transported from Buzz knew not what distant quarry and situated in an oasis so that it had a swimming pool. This latter was a status symbol used solely for such visitors as Buzz himself; the ruler had never been seen in it. And there in the comparative cool Buzz handwrote his seventeen-page report with his fountain pen and the bottle of ink he had purchased at London Airport.

When complete, he read this report aloud to the ruler in his own language, leaving out remarks which would not please him and putting in others which were flowery but had nothing to do with the case.

It was approved, and after that he lay on a lounge garden chair from Harrod's, sucking with a straw from innumerable bottles of Coca-Cola (horribly wind-making) and thinking about his seedlings and plants dying from thirst in Mrs. Furnish's greenhouse. He was wondering, also, how soon he could, with courtesy, leave, because he wished to have at least a week on the way home in Greece, on the tiny island in the archipelago which he and his beloved had called "our Island."

The FO had stipulated three weeks because it could not imagine how the trouble could be settled in less time, but since Buzz was being paid by the ruler in the main and only a nominal fee from the Foreign Office, which was already on the books as payment for a three-week assignment, he felt free to tell the consul in Bahrein of his intentions for the last week, so that if anything were to go wrong at home, they could get in touch with him.

He had parted with the ruler after fourteen days. Sherbia seldom smiled, but at their farewell he clasped his brigadier to his heart and wished him all the good that Allah could shower upon him. And as Buzz was stepping into the Land Rover, the secretary whom he thought of as the grand vizier pressed upon him a check for a disproportionately large amount on a bank in Piccadilly, saying in smooth hissing Arabic the equivalent of "Cash it to avoid income tax!"

A few interested oilmen acquaintances who saw him off at Bahrein airport noted that Buzz Patricott, in spite of his success in Janhara, wore still his habitual look of anxiety.

He had to change planes for Athens, with a four-hour wait at Beirut; time was slowly passing, and he longed for the fresh, yet warm breezes of Greece, when his already artificially chilled skin became roughly bristled with shock. With his dead wife nearly always in mind he knew that hearing her voice, "Buzz darling . . ." immediately behind him was a further step down the road to disintegration. He stared in great depression at the nasty pattern on the terrazzo floor of the waiting hall.

"Buzz . . . how lovely to see you . . ." He looked around; it was his sister-in-law Lucy, wife of a Scottish sheep farmer called Mackay from the hills behind Aberdeen. It was not too surprising that they should meet here because, he remembered, her father had a consular job of long standing in Beirut; he had recently retired and was living at leisure in his delightful villa above the city.

"Hello, Buzz! It's lovely to see you!" It was lovely to see

her, too. He did not consider her to be in the least like his own beloved, but her voice resembled his Jessica's remarkably.

He told her what he had been doing and was about to do; she, too, was waiting for the London plane which would drop Buzz at Athens. He said they had time for a fairly quick lunch, which would be better than having it on the plane.

Both delighted at the encounter, they hurried to the restaurant where Buzz ordered curried duckling and *gesprich*, the iced hock and seltzer that was such a favorite of Oscar Wilde. While they were drinking each other's health and the good fortune at meeting, Lucy said she had been "trying to cheer up Daddy and not really succeeding. I wouldn't let him come to the airport; he has taken Fatty's death very hard, poor darling."

Fatty was the childhood name which had stuck forever with one of her sons, called Patrick, who had been a stout small boy. Since the brigadier had no idea that Patrick was ill, let alone dead, he was shocked.

"It was two months ago, Buzz darling; didn't you see it in the papers? Patrick Mackay!"

"God! That bomb explosion in Northern Ireland!"

"That was it."

"Of course, of course, Patrick something or other Mackay. . . ."

"Patrick James Bonner Mackay, his paternal grandmother's name, aged nineteen. . . ."

He beat his temples. "I never thought of him as anything but Fatty." He leaned across the table. "Oh, Lucy! How terrible!" He took her hand.

"Don't, don't sympathize, I shall cry."

"I never heard, or wrote, or anything. . . ."

"We haven't opened any of the letters yet, we can't."

"I could have rung up . . ." he started, but realized how very much it would not have mattered to them whether he had telephoned or not, at the time.

It was as well he had ordered a light meal; neither of them could do more than pick at it; breaking the news all over again brought back the event too strongly for her to eat much.

She reminded Buzz how keen a horseman their youngest boy had always been and how, even as a small boy, he had won prizes at horsemanship, and he had been so keen to "go into the horse industry," as his father called it. This Fatty had taken himself off to a famous stud in Northern Ireland, where he had been working happily for nine months or so. With a friend one Saturday evening they had gone into Belfast to see a cowboy film and then, late at night, on the way back through the side streets to their car, a bomb had been thrown, killing one and severely wounding the other. The other boy had only just come out of hospital, having almost lost his sight. ". . . Fatty was killed instantly, mercifully."

"All so unnecessary. . . ."

They mourned.

In due course their flight number was called, and they made their way to the London plane.

"Isn't it a strange thing?" Buzz said when they were seated. "I've been shocked by this terrible news of yours, and now I am conforting my mind with: Well, they have two more fine boys!"

He turned to see the effect of this; she shook her head sadly. "You can't afford to lose *one* child, however many more you have."

And then after a while he said: "And now I've actually been thinking: It's just one of those things."

She nodded again. "But what things?"

"Is this worse . . . or better . . . than that he should have been killed driving too fast in a car?"

She thought for a long time, fiddling with her seat belt and watching the latecomers hurrying across the scorching tarmac. "It's worse, Buzz; on the whole, it is worse."

"I must confess," Buzz murmured, "that I personally never give much attention to the Irish thing; it's like fleas in the trenches, it's something you have, regrettably, but always with you. This Irish thing has been going on about a hundred years. Peer back into the last century and there it

107

is . . . going on . . . We've given the Irish back most of their damned country . . . why can't we give them back the rest of it? It's only six counties, after all."

"Oh, Buzz!" she almost screamed. "It's not like that. Oh, darling! You are funny . . . it is much more complicated. They're not a tiny country in central Africa . . . they . . . in a way . . . they're *us!*"

Seat belts were fastened, engines revved up.

"We've talked enough about us and our tragedy. What about you, darling?" She turned and looked fully at him as though for the first time. "How are you doing?"

"Well, I'm struggling with the part of father without any great success. I've got this small job working in a hothouse, as I told you in my Christmas letter. . . . I've got a nice woman who does the housework," he added carefully, "and some cooking. The boys go to a local 'comprehensive,' but they ought to be at boarding school, since a home without a mother is no great shakes. They're becoming great pigeon fanciers; that's their hobby, very much encouraged by the fancier living in the big house of which we occupy the lodge. . . . They need discipline, though, and a father trying to be kind and make up for no mother isn't the one to provide it."

"You're a soldier, darling. . . ."

"It's not the same kind of discipline. God! I'm damned bad at it, I'm cowardly, you see, I want them to like me, so I daren't discipline them." He held up his left hand and stared at it with dislike. "I'm a weak coward, and I know it! I know disciplinarians are needed today, and I know that the young respect them, I know all that, but I am too cowardly and weak and stupid and sentimental . . . in my mind's eye they are still darling little giggling ticklable fatties, like your Fatty, and *I can't get it out of my system.*"

His sister-in-law tucked her arm through his and pressed his side.

"And aren't you ever going to marry again, Buzz?"

"If you mean marry to give the boys a mother? Certainly not. The boys grow up and leave home and you're left with the damned mother!"

She laughed a little but not much.

"Don't you want to have a wife, as a wife, a companion in bed?"

"No, I don't. Somehow or other, I know I'm half-baked, but sex without love doesn't, doesn't do anything for me."

There was a long pause while the plane flattened out and mealy words came from the loudspeaker; everybody unfastened his seat belt.

"I'll be leaving you soon, Lucy!" He turned to her, looking at her charming face. "I always hate having to say good-bye to you. I hardly ever see you and John, do I? We're living in a very modest way indeed; the lodge at the gates of an erstwhile small mansion; you wouldn't like it much. This trip is like a bus ride, really, from Beirut to Athens, no sooner up than down!"

"So you're going to have a week sitting on your island thinking about your Jessica . . . how I wish you didn't have to! I do wish I knew somebody . . . there's lots of lonely women about . . . if only. . . ."

"Thanks, darling, but don't bother. I'm all right. I've someone *on* my bed, if not in. My dear little Yorkshire Maggie, at this moment lying on my eiderdown, not moving a hair in case she misses the first sound of my return. . . ."

They both laughed.

"I'm not going to our island to wallow in sentiment, I promise you. I'm going for that lovely warm breeze and that dashing sea—you should have seen me floundering about in the sheikh's hot, sticky pool!—and the only place I know where the food is really, really something in that pub on our island which has no more than twelve guests. You and John should go for a holiday there and heal your wounds. . . ."

When the few travelers leaving the plane at Athens got up and pulled down their hand baggage, he bent forward to kiss his sister-in-law good-bye, but she could not turn her face to him because she was crying.

He pressed her arm. "I promise I won't just be sitting thinking about Jessica . . . I'll be thinking about the IRA and the troubles in Ireland."

What am I carrying this thing all over the place *for?* he

asked himself as he pulled out from under the seat the roll of Persian rug, wrapped carefully in sacking, which had been the sheikh's last gift. It had only just been allowed as hand luggage, and he had been suitably grateful to the stewardess for complying.

He put it on the seat he had vacated and pushed it against his sister-in-law. "A present for you, Lucy, for you and John, to brighten up your northern castle."

Still she did not look around; her face was hidden in her handkerchief, so he whipped out his fountain pen and wrote on the label her name and address. He hurried away from the plane without looking back.

13

The thinking had to start. But it takes time for the wholly innocent to realize that they might appear guilty. It looked very much as though he had escaped from the difficult situation at home, but it was the check which now lay beside him on the beach—in his notecase of which he never lost sight—a fraction of it, in anticipation, which had caused him to make the decision to come to the assistance of Janhara.

The love of money is the root of all evil, so they say, but Buzz told himself he hated money, really hated it. It was just so damnable that he needed money to conduct his life in what he considered the best way. Mrs. Furnish's money would have been no good to him at all; it would have cost too much in human dignity, but this sum he had achieved from the sheikh was money honorably earned and brought, therefore, satisfaction, or rather—the spending of it would.

But nevertheless, to leave the situation at home with a clear admission of having spent his last hours with a murdered woman was questionable. What was more subject to examination was his two rapid changes of mind; first, he had gone to London to say he would not go to Janhara, and second, after the body had been found, he decided that he would, after all, go, with two minor changes of mind in between. Vacillation is hardly a covering word for volte-face.

Only a simpleton would fool about in the way he had done and expect to be behaving normally. But then, he was a simpleton; he had always known that he gave that impression. His round face and his round eyes and his general mien were that of a simpleton, together with his left-handedness, so that when he picked up a pen to sign anything, he looked more daft than deft. Lying on a glorious Greek beach, with a warm wind blowing over him, he considered himself a far from heroic sight. Though his tummy did not exactly hide from his view the blue bathing drawers, his general tubbiness was not such as to cause anyone to turn and look a second time at him.

It was no good being depressed about something which was unavoidable, but he had to realize that a man who looked right was much more likely to override an extremely questionable situation such as he found himself in than a man, like himself, whose physical appearance did not inspire confidence. And even under the bluest of blue skies his name annoyed him. Admittedly, to be called *Buzz* was better than *Baz*, but why did he inspire a slightly jokey diminutive at all, why not plain Basil?

His lonely childhood had been colored and enhanced by heroes; his father had been a soldier, winning the MC and DSC and dying gloriously (if uselessly) at Dunkirk; there was a photograph of him on his mother's dressing table: a fine tall fellow who as a callow youth had won the King's Sword at Sandhurst. Basil's only ambition had been to follow his father, even to the dying gloriously.

Things being the way they were, there was nothing these days to die gloriously about, and he had shown an aptitude for foreign languages which the army had been pleased to encourage. But he remained dissatisfied, even though his proficiency in Arabic was still often extremely useful; he called himself a backroom boy, and the mental picture of himself as a cavalry officer in the Light Brigade, slashing

111

with his saber to right and to left, felling the enemy by the dozen as he rode straight for the cannon's mouth, was relegated to dreams after a heavy meal.

He forced himself to think about Mrs. Furnish. "Call me Desirée," she had said so often, and try as he might, he could not bring the word out of his mouth. What had the poor thing ever done to make one dislike her? Why, even, did one think of her as "the poor thing"? As far as one could see she had "everything that anyone could want."

Except that she had nothing . . . nothing that mattered, only the things perhaps that the color supplements seem to consider to matter, cars and diamonds and the right whiskey.

As far as the Patricott father and sons were concerned, she had done nothing but good; she had been immensely kind. She had found them the little house to rent, had rustled up workmen to repair and decorate, guided them to the right shops and finally offered him a job such as his heart yearned for. Wincing, he laid his head upon his arms on the coarse silver sand and moaned. In spite of all this . . . they hated her; the boys did, anyway. He tolerated her.

How can you hate somebody because of his voice?

His teeth?

The way he walks?

You can moan with the misery of it, but it doesn't help to say: But inside there's a lovely person struggling to get out. (Or inside that fat little brigadier, there's a handsome hero struggling to get out.)

He got up and dashed into the sea again; there was nobody in sight; to the far left the group of white cottages constituted the town and the "hotel"; there were colorful boats bobbing about at anchor and fishermen's nets drying on the beach; they had been working on them all morning and had gone indoors for their meal.

He came out of the sparkling sea in a businesslike mood with the real thinking started. Never mind the hideous scene in the kitchen; what had happened after he left? He had asked the police almost as many questions as they had asked him. She must have tidied up the kitchen and locked the kitchen door; she had gone back to the drawing room because, in the morning, the lights had been on still and the electric fire. The curtains had been drawn close, he had remembered noticing with a sinking heart that she drew them as soon as they had come in. There were no signs of any struggle; the hall light was on and the *front door unlocked*.

In his opinion that pointed to a visit from someone she knew; it might well have been someone she had seen in court as a magistrate; she was not the nervous type of woman who would not open the door to anyone late at night. Or it might have been a friend. And if it was a friend, they would all be at a loss, because who was to know exactly what friends she had?

It was not somebody to whom she had given a drink from the drinks tray, because the two brandy glasses they had used, Buzz and Mrs. Furnish, were in the kitchen sink.

She had been found sitting in the large knowle sofa. These sofas were uncomfortable things; Buzz had never found it possible either to lie or to sit in one at ease, but they were a relic of a period when it was very okay to have one. The back and sides rose two or three feet above the cushioned seat and the two corners were tied by thick silk cords to keep them together, so that if the ropes became loose there was enough space between side and back to cause a howling draft at the back of the neck of anyone sitting there. She had been sitting at the left side of the settee, to anyone standing before the fireplace, as Buzz had. And she had been shot through the head twice—that is, her right side would be protected from a gunshot by the tall sofa's side, but her left side, the heart side, would be vulnerable. She would not have been seated if someone had walked through the front door; she would have gone to see who it was. Therefore, she knew the murderer, brought him in and sat down upon the sofa, and must have been talking to him when he drew out the gun and shot her, point-blank. He had had the gun ready; indeed, he may have come to the house with the object of shooting her.

This was all circumstantial evidence; when Buzz had arrived upon the scene, the body had been removed to the ambulance, but the police officer had picked up a cushion and placed it exactly where the body had been found, sitting slumped but upright.

Presumptive evidence is the same as circumstantial evidence; when one fact has been proved, the existence of another fact may naturally be inferred. These *presumptions of fact* are what keep defense counsel in business, because they stand good only until proved incorrect.

And another niggling thought had been actively laying eggs in the back of Buzz's mind and that was . . . *conclusive presumptions.* Some of these had had a nasty knock in the so-called permissive society of today. One was that a child of eight is incapable of committing a crime. Not that a child of eight came into his problem, but two children of ten and twelve did. Children developed at an earlier age now than in the past; he did not think of his own boys as particularly clever, but they were enormously advanced upon himself at their age. They were so knowing, that was what distressed him so greatly; they knew everything.

They probably knew, for instance, whereabouts in the lodge he kept his revolver, now lying on the beach beside his notecase in the small string locally made bathing bag. They could have taken the revolver before his return home on the Friday evening and gone to the Red House with it as he was driving back in the Rolls, home to bed. On their return, they could have replaced it behind the books where he had always kept it.

Eight miles?

How did they travel the eight miles to the Red House?

They had no means of transport.

But they were so fiendishly knowing that he was frightened.

They detested Mrs. Furnish as a menace to their solidarity. "She's going to marry Father, and our lives will be hell!" That was enough motive. Fantastic, mad, wild imaginings verging on insanity. But then, open the newspaper any day and read of fantastic happenings.

"That could never happen to us!"

Could it not?

Since a clue to the death of his benefactress could well

lie in what had passed between them, he had to think over the evening in detail, however much he might wish it all to pass into oblivion, and when it came to the scene in the kitchen, he writhed visibly and mentally, lying on his stomach in the sand and kicking up his heels as he had done when embarrassed as a small boy. Tearing her arms from around his neck, in a burst of annoyance, and his cry of terror, as from the same small boy—"I don't want to marry you, please don't make me!"—should never appear upon memory's slate. Her subsequent abuse of him did not injure him, but, dear God! it hurt her; her gentlewoman's facade not only slipped, it fell off altogether, her dignity and good fellowship . . . all, all vanished; he stood aghast, facing a harridan. It was almost impossible not to remember her like that, forgetting the previous kindness and thoughtfulness and general beneficence. It was a great pity that he should be left with this sickening memory.

And what had she been trying to tell him about O'Duff? He could only imagine that she had thought him a pederast and wished to warn him of danger to the boys, and that sickened him, too.

He turned over on his side, looking toward the "village" in the shimmering distance, and laid his head upon his arm. Three people were coming toward him; at this distance they looked abnormally tall and thin; he had noticed this phenomenon often and had enjoyed Lowry's pictures because the artist recognized it so strongly and put it to artistic use.

In Greece it takes three or more people to deliver a telegram—one person to carry the missive and two or more to come along as observers of the hoped-for drama which might follow delivery to the recipient.

Dreamily, Buzz watched them approaching and, as they did, becoming less and less like stick men the nearer they came. They were coming to him; he sat up to receive them.

The FO had kept faithful track of him; he stretched out his hand for the telegram: NOT TO PANIC BUT ADVISE YOUR RETURN HOME AS SOON AS POSSIBLE, FLOWER. His physical well-being at that moment was so good that his face did not instantly reassume its worried expression. His eyes looked very blue in his tanned face; he even smiled at his expectant audience. "Nobody's died, but I'm afraid I'll have to go home."

Speculation was mind-breaking: Which of the boys? What cast-iron piece of evidence had appeared of the boys' involvement in the murder of Mrs. Furnish? NOT TO PANIC? It did not mean death or even imminent death. Would she consider, for instance, the death or disappearance of a miniature Yorkshire terrier bitch worth a telegram? No. It was worse, much worse.

Short of an anesthetic to make the journey home bearable, alcohol was the only other possible amelioration of the anguish. But not ouzo. At Athens Airport he bought half a bottle of whiskey which he could slip into his raincoat pocket. He sat down in a comfortable armchair with a tumbler beside him and watched the people passing.

He thought about his young nephew, the victim of a revolution, and he thought about the prevalence of revolutions and how they cropped up here and there, all over the world, and how he had warned Sherbia's brother: "Keep peace amongst yourselves for the love of Allah; professional revolutionaries wait outside the camp; in a tiny community like yours, your solidarity is essential; through small cracks in your stability the paid international rabblerousers creep in, those who appear wherever there is the smell of revolution, like rats in an unclean slaughterhouse. Your best friend is your brother NO MATTER WHAT, and if you disagree in your heart, you must override that disagreement. As men with but a single thought you are strong, as quarreling over any matter whatever you are nothing and nobody but a herd of bewildered, disintegrating Bedouin."

What splendid, rolling phrases these sounded in Arabic! A glow of pride flowed over him with only one quarter of the half bottle consumed. Yet how uncertain he was, how pitifully vacillating and inadequate he not only felt but was, in the conduct of his daily life. How deplorable and stupid it was to spend a moment bothering about being left-handed; how introspective and time-wasting. To the

116

Bedouin he said the right thing without even stopping to think, yet in the countryside of his own homeland he was a nervously twitching, pitiful object.

He had forgotten what he was hurrying home about as he crossed to the waiting plane. Usually he hated the lonely walk across the tarmac, lonely with dozens of others. He always felt they were a tiny group detaching themselves from Mother Earth to fly out into the universe, very fast, and unlikely to return. But now, carrying his raincoat, with a new unopened half bottle in his pocket, and his dispatch case swinging as gaily as a schoolboy's satchel, he gave a small skip up the steps of the plane with no more anxiety than if he were catching the twenty-seven bus for Paddington.

Later, the hostess' face was very sweet, so near him he longed to kiss it. He wanted to say: "You're very sweet," but instead he said: "You can take a white horse anywhere. . . ."

She dealt with him divinely, which is what hostesses are for, and in an amazingly short time he found himself sitting in a second-class carriage passing through Slough. Looking up, he saw his leather case on the rack above him, beside him his dispatch case and his raincoat, and, oddly enough the *Evening Standard,* neatly unopened.

"What day is it?" he asked the ticket collector in a low voice.

It was Wednesday.

Dinner was being served in the restaurant car, so it must be evening. He felt very empty, so he went along the corridor and had a meal.

No one met him at the station because they did not know when he was coming. He took the station taxi home.

James and Mrs. Flower rushed to meet him as he climbed out and paid the driver.

Joshua was missing, and that was the sum of it; there was just a shade of anticlimax about it because Joshua had been missing once or twice before but not for nearly so long.

On Saturday last . . . the big pigeon race and Joshua left alone with the clock to record the heroine's flight home. James and Mr. O'Duff had come back from the pigeon club to find no Joshua and no returned pigeon. James had

117

gone home to bed, tired out, and had slept undisturbed all night.

In the meantime Mrs. Flower had come home well before ten o'clock from her visit to her old aunt and gone to bed and to sleep. That she should have waited up for the boys' return and failed to do so was a cause of great concern and grief to her, but would it have made any difference?

Sunday morning and the police were alerted. *Sunday evening* and they were not only alerted but called in and became concerned.

Monday and a search party was formed. Late on Monday the telegram was sent after a call to the Foreign Office.

Tuesday, search party called off, it being considered that Joshua had "run away from home." Could be for a variety of reasons, all of which were brought up by the police and discussed with Mrs. Flower.

Joshua's description circulated in a countrywide memo to all police stations. James did not return to school because he hated the publicity, and also because Mrs. Flower needed some support, Maggie needed some exercise and the pigeons needed looking after.

Mr. O'Duff was full of the grimmest forebodings, because he said he had found the back door wide open on his return from the club. He had, of course, locked up and taken the key when he had left with James, but the spare key had gone from under the plant pot in the shed and was in the door. And nobody, but nobody, except perhaps Mr. O'Duff's brother Cart, gone back to Ireland, knew of the whereabouts of that key, and they knew because on one occasion Mr. O'Duff had been collecting a pigeon basket from somewhere and had left behind his raincoat, in the pocket of which was the key of the house. Thoughtlessly, as it turned out, he had been heaving the basket across the yard and shouted to Joshua to fetch the hidden key from under the plant pot in the potting shed. Later he had fetched his raincoat from where he had left it and had even more thoughtlessly returned the key to the place in which it had been hidden, rather than find a new place about which nobody knew but himself. Mr. O'Duff was almost mortally stricken with grief at his own carelessness over the key; it struck him, it would seem, as far more important than Joshua's actual disappearance. He described himself as "falling over backwards" in his search of the house, just in case Joshua should be "playing naughty" and hiding from them all. From attics to cellars, not a square inch was left unexamined, he assured everyone.

In fact, Joshua's disappearance was almost carelessly tossed off by him because are not young people constantly disappearing from their homes? Joshua was an independent lad; he had a mind of his own, that child. He might have "run away to sea"; this last was a funny old concept which dated Mr. O'Duff considerably. Young people might still run away to "seek their fortune" (possibly), now called "doing your own thing," but not to pig it in a tramp steamer, well, hardly ever, not in an affluent society.

"Where do you think Joshua has gone, James? Tell me honestly, you must have some ideas. Think hard."

"I've been thinking, Father, very, very hard."

"Have you come to any conclusion? Don't say: *I don't know*, I know you don't know, but have you any ideas? Josh is an imaginative child, you both are, partly due to your varied early youth, perhaps, foreign travel; perhaps it's all made your minds work overtime."

"He may be dead, Father. He may have had the idea of going somewhere suddenly and thumbed a lift and . . . got murdered."

"That was something you read in the papers last month."

"He might have gone to Ireland to have a look round, find a leprechaun, perhaps. Mr. O'Duff is forever talking about Ireland and singing these songs about the Mountains of Mourne and all that. . . ."

"Jabberwocky. . . ."

"I bet he'll send a postcard from some fantastic place, just to surprise us."

"But he hasn't any money!"

"You left us a pound between us for each week you were away."

The brigadier jumped up, collecting Maggie from his

knee and tucking her under his arm, and walked up and down the living room. Sometimes his boys made remarks that he found unbearably touching. "He couldn't go very far on that, old chap."

James hardly heard. "But it's worrying, isn't it? Josh was much too keen on the pigeons to go away at the moment, anyway. He wanted to be with them and doing things for them every minute of the day; he hated even going to school because he had to leave the pigeons. And there's the two new ones the Duffer gave us . . . in the paddock. . . ."

And now Buzz said the unsayable, let alone the unthinkable. He said: "Did Josh shoot Mrs. Furnish with my gun, James?"

Unastonished James said no, not with anybody else's gun either. "Did you shoot her, Father?"

"No, James, I didn't. But I had a horrid row with her in what may have been within the same hour she was shot."

"About marrying her?"

"Yah . . ." Complete understanding prevailed; if they had never done so before, they loved each other then.

14

But Joshua had to be found; nobody would believe that he was lying strangled in a ditch as other little boys have been.

His father said that Joshua was an intractable child, independent and with a mind which he used. This intractability was sometimes hard to bear; it was grieving to learn that from time to time one had to give in to Joshua's lack of cooperation, and there had been many times when the brigadier had had to croak in a tired voice: "Well, perhaps you're right, Joshua." Remembering these episodes was a comfort; Joshua was not one to be docile with some mad pervert, tempting him with car rides,

120

chocolates, meals or treats; he would be rude as only he could be when he wanted, as they all knew to their cost; he could be offhand and, if pressed, just plain determined not to comply.

In retrospect the afternoon and evening of his disappearance was a curious one, but it must be admitted that it became curious only when things had gone wrong. Mrs. Flower *had* gone to see her aunt but this had been done before; Joshua had often been left alone at the lodge watching the television, or reading, or cleaning the loft. There had been times when Buzz and his elder son had gone somewhere that Joshua did not want to go and returned late to find Joshua in bed asleep or reading.

The brigadier had to reassure Mrs. Flower over and over again that there was no blame resting upon her. In Mrs. Flower's opinion a lot of rum people came and went up and down the drive; there was abnormal activity, she thought, and she would like to know what kind of business Mr. O'Duff up at the house was carrying on. Oh, he was pleasant enough but. . . .

"But what, Mrs. Flower?"

She did not answer.

"Any idea anybody has, however absurd it may seem, should come out into the open. So come on, Mrs. Flower, but what?"

"You know what they're like, love! Charming and friendly and ever so nice . . . but what are they up to, these very Irish men?"

"How do you mean, up to?"

"Something for themselves. . . ."

"Come, come, Mrs. Flower. They're all right, it's only the extremists . . ." and at the word "extremists" Buzz received a piercing stab of memory. Circumstances and whiskey had wiped his mind clear of the journey home.

"James! I met your Aunt Lucy at Beirut Airport on my way to Greece; she'd been seeing her father and was on her way back home, to Scotland. Oh, what do you think, James? Fatty has been killed, killed accidentally by a bomb explosion in Belfast . . . not that it was all that accidental; what am I saying? When bombs go off, someone gets killed, and it had to be he who stopped some of it, and the chap he was with terribly injured."

James, never seen to cry, cried. He cried twice as hard as he might have cried, crying not only for his cousin but for his brother whom he was now sure he would never see again. He went on for a long time, and they let him; it was good for him.

For their training flights the old birds went with the young. Mr. O'Duff packed a dozen in each of two baskets and took them to his favorite throwing site in his Mercedes. There he threw them into the air and hurried back home, standing in the yard waiting for them. It was somehow a heart-leaping sight for the oldest to the youngest of fanciers to see them swoop in in one lovely tight unit, moving as one entity, around, away out into the near sky, and here again in seconds in perfect ordinance; in his relation to them he was like a man with a kite, having absolute control over them. He held his head up and watched them; his face might well have lighted up acknowledging the existence of the small glory of it; and when they flew straight across the yard immediately over his head, recognizing him in their form of salute, he did not cry aloud with pleasure, but his upper lip lengthened, and his face with that jutting chin looked more than ever like the map of Ireland.

The brigadier went up to the big house alone. Mr. O'Duff had just shut up his birds. He found no lack of sympathy there; Mr. O'Duff's face could be said to be in mourning, it was indeed a shade or two darker and his manner likewise. It was raining slightly, and Buzz was carrying Maggie, since that little bitch did not wish to get her feet wet, and in spite of the rain, Mr. O'Duff came out of the stable and into the yard, carrying a bucket as usual and closing the door carefully behind him.

"You'll forgive me not asking you in, Brigadier, sorr, but you know what it's like in a house with no woman in it. The mess." There was no laugh; he stood before the brigadier, looking at him with mournful, haggard eyes. "I've not had a wink of sleep since the boy disappeared. I'll guarantee you haven't either, eh? Oh, it's a cruel, hard thing to bear. . . ." His voice having taken on the blood-curdling keening note, Buzz longed to get away, but resolutely stayed where he stood, the collar of his raincoat turned up and with Maggie shriveled to her smallest version of herself so that there was less of her to get wet.

Buzz had no idea what sort of terms he was on with this curious person, and if there had been a thunderstorm, he would have stayed where he stood, uninvited into shelter. This man who had so much to do with his boys, at whom he had never really looked, came, suddenly, into focus. "Shambling" and "sluttish" were the first two adjectives that sprang into his mind, but there was a lot more to him than that, which was baffling.

"I want to talk to you . . ." Buzz said almost in a dream, bewildered.

Mr. O'Duff stepped closer, ready to stand out in the rain and talk, but clearly was not going to open his door and invite him in.

"A friend of ours, of mine, was murdered the day before I had to go away."

A great cry interrupted him. "As if I didn't know that! She was around here the very afternoon she was shot. I don't know how great a friend of yours she was, Brigadier, though I do know a good deal from your boys, but if she made a habit of going round folks' houses when they're out, I'd say she deserved what she got!"

"Surely not! Surely not inside your house, Mr. O'Duff?"

"Well"—he gesticulated with his hands—"one way or the other, it hardly matters. I was only in the loft with my beauties."

Buzz snapped that there was quite a big difference; was she *inside?* Since it seemed to be that she was not, he said he could perfectly understand her having a look around the *outside* of the house; it was a very attractive, interesting building, a perfect example of the domestic architecture of its period, he would no doubt have had others looking round the *outside* with interest. He added dangerously: "The fact that you keep it so securely locked makes it more intriguing." And he added even more oddly: "No one would be surprised to see a couple of machine guns mounted either side of the front door." It wasn't much of a joke, and it fell out of Buzz's mouth carelessly, as it were, straight from his subconscious, without any reference to current thought. He was shocked into silence which he could only break with the most artificial and unreal giggle he had ever produced.

The things that were happening to Mr. O'Duff's face defy description, owing to the speed with which the scene seemed to change and rechange.

"You see, Mr. O'Duff," he went on cursively, "it is essential to look at every aspect of my boy's disappearance . . . we had this cold-blooded murder three weeks ago with which I was very closely connected. We haven't had the inquest yet, but, my word, you'll be surprised how closely I was connected with it when you read it all in the local paper. I am to be the chief witness. Three weeks after this murder . . . my boy disappears, *my* boy. The obvious question arises. . . ."

"Nart at all, nart at all . . . I know your young Joshua very well indeed, better I venture to say, sorr, than you know him yourself. There's a barrier between father and sons there, you'll be the first to admit. You are . . . now what is the word, *baffled*, by them, isn't that so?"

Mr. O'Duff was taller than he; Buzz had to raise his chin slightly to look into his face. He did not do that, but looked down on the top of Maggie's pale gold and silver head, which he tickled with one finger.

"I'm very, very fond of those boys of yours. I find them real good company, an old gaffer like me! They put life in me, it's nice to have the young about, I haven't quite forgotten what it is to be young. . . ." The brigadier, of course, had, lay unspoken upon the damp air.

"Josh is bursting with brains . . . he's off to see the world!"

"At nine?"

"Yes, at nine rising ten, why nart?"

"If he'd been a few years older I'd have agreed, but not Josh. I grant he's incredibly advanced for his years, owing to all the travel they have been forced to experience, left

124

alone for hours in furnished flats in Middle East towns, and all that . . . travel has become tiresome to those boys of mine. The things they enjoy most have been provided by you . . ." and he repeated: "By you!"

Mr. O'Duff had been holding a cigarette with the hand not gripping the galvanized bucket. He held it inward, smoking into his palm, in the way some people do as though hiding it in shame from the observer. Now it had burned down to his fingers, and with a slight hiss of pain he threw it down and stamped upon it, fallen upon the wet cobblestones of the old stable yard.

"Well now, sorr, if your boy isn't run away from home, there's other things you have to consider. Everyone knows you're in the Secret Service. . . ." He raised a hand to silence the protest that instantly broke from the brigadier. "Wait a minute, wait a minute . . . everybody round about knows you're off doing government business, all very secret, every now and then. And look! The day before you last went away, the very day after your lady friend was shot dead in her bed, no it wasn't her bed was it, it was the parlor sofa . . . the day after, these colorful characters turned up in this great American car looking for Brigadier Patricott, right here in the front drive they were and a funny color they were too, neither black nor white!"

"God! You nitwit!" Buzz shouted. "It doesn't matter what damned color they were . . . perfectly normal ordinary people . . . just not European, that's all. . . ."

Mr. O'Duff put down the bucket and raised both hands to soothe the brigadier.

"No offense, no offense intended, but I just wanted to point out. . . ."

"Point out what?"

'Mr. O'Duff shook his head slowly from side to side. "There's . . . been . . . some . . . funny goings-on. I won't go on because it doesn't please Yer Honor, but I must in all fairness point out that the lady Furnish was a magistrate."

"What does that prove?" Buzz asked indignantly.

"I'm not saying it proves anything, but it needs thinking about. . . ."

There was a long pause, almost a truce, during which time Buzz's anger ran out of the heels of his Wellington boots.

"Look," he said at long last, "I apologize. . . ."

"That's all right, Brigadier sorr, that's all right by me," Mr. O'Duff said readily, too readily. "Don't give it another thought. I know how you feel, it's a worry, a very great worry you have on your mind . . . your little boy adrift in a wicked world. . . ."

Apologetic though he was, Buzz's nerves were badly on edge; he had to interrupt the flow of sympathy. "I mean"—he changed Maggie to the other arm; he felt suddenly terribly tired—"I mean . . . in a lifetime of reasonable security, my boys, I mean *and* myself as a family . . . we suddenly have two violent happenings . . . well, the second one may be *violent* or prove not to be in the end . . . but these two happenings within a short time of one another, the shooting of Mrs. Furnish, with which, as I say, I am closely connected, and the disappearance of my boy . . . one cannot but wonder what, if any, is the connection."

"The boys have been to the Red House while you were away, and more than once," Mr. O'Duff reported, and his face wore the exact expression as worn by the sneak going to headmaster to report misconduct among his formmates. The brigadier thought his face ridiculously overexpressive, like a ham actor; he toyed with the idea of warning him against ever playing poker and adding the advice that he should stick to snap!

Instead he asked for further information.

When Mrs. Thingummy, down at the lodge, the lady who looks after them, when her son came to his home for the weekend he took them all out to the Red House. They went to water the plants in the greenhouse, they told him, all the seedlings, an innocent enough trip, Mr. O'Duff considered it to be, with a ghastly frown, his eyebrows coming down so far that they practically obliterated his eyes altogether. He added: "But what happened there?"

Almost dizzy, Buzz held his forehead with his free hand and struggled to make some sort of order of his bewildered thoughts. He had not given much thought to his greenhouse; he could hardly remember what he was doing there at all; it all seemed such a long way off, so long ago.

"What sort of thing could have happened there? Mrs. Flower, her son and the boys? What sort of thing have you in mind? They wouldn't have to break in; I left a key to the greenhouse hanging in our little lobby."

Mr. O'Duff spread his hands in bewilderment. "You say everything has to be taken into account, every movement considered, I was only. . . ." He shrugged again. "But you're quite right, Brigadier . . . you're right to do your own thinking. The police are too busy with their motoring offenses to take too much time over law and order. . . ."

"I shouldn't say that if I were you!" Buzz warned. "It might bring you bad luck!"

". . . so you have to be your own private detective these days and good luck to you! I admire you for it!"

Buzz's teeth were set on edge. There was something about the man which made him want to knock him flat, and this he could easily have done, in spite of his height. He looked him up and down, sorely tempted.

Mr. O'Duff must have guessed at the brigadier's frame of mind. He held his hands out in a protective manner and moved slightly away. "I understand how you feel, I feel just the same . . . I love that boy like he was my own son I nivver had."

Buzz looked away to avoid temptation. "What about the bird, the racer?"

Mr. O'Duff looked as puzzled as though he had never set eyes on any bird; then with a loud cry of comprehension, he shouted: "You mean me racing pigeon? Oh, Brigadier sorr, I've thought meself silly about that. I can't understand it, it's quite beyond me comprehension. Josh was as fond of the birds as I am meself, and he was proud to be left watching for the fly-in, with the good clock and all. There was no prouder small boy within the length and breadth of the kingdom, left on the watch whilst I took his brother off to the club to see the fun that end . . . I can only believe he got bored waiting . . . that's the only answer as I see it."

"That doesn't sound credible at all. . . ."

127

Mr. O'Duff shook his head. "Not at all at all! I don't know what to make of it no more than you."

"Is the bird lost?"

"Would you believe it now, I found it feeding with the others on Sunday morning, the racing ring still on its claw. I'd the trap open for exercise as I always do, and she must have flown in when me back was turned. Disqualified, of course, which was a pity, she's me finest bird and stood a good chance of winning that first race of the season. . . ."

"What does it mean, then? That Joshua was not there when it arrived?"

"There's times when they, the birds, I mean, play the fool on arriving back; if the trapdoor isn't opened instantly to let them in, they'll play hard to get, fool about. You see, they don't realize they're in a race, not like a horse who knows the lot. All they know is they've got to get home to their pad. Instinct, the homing instinct, you must have heard of that! Jealousy! They want their mate, and they want home, and they'll fly a thousand miles in a howling gale to get back . . . it's exciting, eh?"

It might be exciting, but Buzz was in no mood to discuss it at length.

Mr. O'Duff grumbled that his bird would be a goner for any more racing, this year anyway; it had flown back from where it was transported by truck, in a basket, with lots of others also in baskets . . . it had flown back all this way only to find the door shut in its face! The shame of it now grew to such proportions that the shame of Joshua's plight seemed to shrivel to insignificance. He was bursting with indignation for his bird.

Buzz could no longer strive to be civil. He turned and walked away down the drive, putting Maggie down to trot at his heels.

15

There were no meals going; Mrs. Flower had not totally disintegrated but was in a state of shock and despair; soggy with tears and distraught, she spent her time standing at the sink washing innumerable articles which she must have dragged out from antique cabin trunks and tin uniform cases which had belonged to Buzz's grandfather, with the name R. C. Patricott painted in neat white, now greatly chipped, lettering. Baby clothes, even, were stored in these, and numerous articles of clothing of Buzz's dead wife; mindlessly she washed and hung out to dry and finally ironed and put back the lot.

In London, in merciful oblivion, Buzz's mother played bridge, paced smilingly through the Army and Navy Stores and went alone to see a revival of *The Chalk Garden*, which she had seen in such happy circumstances once long, long ago. Buzz could not bring himself to telephone to his mother until Joshua had been found. Until?

"Come with me to the Red House, James?"

Willingly James rose from the squatting position in which he had been scrubbing out the bucket used for mixing pigeon food. He dried his hands on the side of his jeans and climbed into the pickup. In silence they drove until, turning into the drive, Buzz groaned; a police car was standing outside the house. "Not still here!"

They drove around the side and went into the hothouse. The heating had been off since Buzz had left, so he was not expecting much, but some of the hardier plants had survived, even flourished, and some of the seedlings were more than ready to be potted. He started work at once, saying that he had thought the house would be deserted and that he very much wanted another look around the rooms they had been in "that night," hoping that he might be reminded of something, however small, that he had forgotten or overlooked.

Some of the potted plants had been rearranged; the pelargoniums had been arranged, banked up, beside the water tank. "Joshua did that," James pointed out. "He said it saved labor to have them all banked up near the water; it took him ages to carry them along there."

Buzz smiled. "Typical of Joshua; his was an adventurous spirit!"

James stood looking at him sadly. "*Was*, Father?"

Buzz went on planting and did not look up. "We've got to face it, it might well be . . . *was*."

James turned away to hide his face.

Buzz went on in a flat voice: "It happens to other people; we're not special, why shouldn't it happen to us? Other people have to bear things that are unbearable, so why not us?"

Presently James moved closer. "The bobby is watching us," he murmured.

"Which one?" Buzz murmured without looking up.

"The chief inspector one. . . ."

"Don't look. . . ."

He continued steadily, if less steadily, to plant out, and after a tiresomely long time, the chief inspector opened the door and came into the comparative warmth.

"Ah, Inspector?"

"I'm sorry we have no news for you, Brigadier, sorry indeed."

"I've been wondering, Chief Inspector. . . ."

"Yes, sir, wondering is no bad thing, no bad thing at all. Stop wondering and you lose contact, I sometimes say to the lads." He waited to be told about the wondering, but now that it came to it, to tell his thoughts only showed up their feebleness. Buzz hesitated for quite a long time.

"Has . . . has the daughter arrived?"

"Shortly before your return, an American lady, a Mrs. Gruntz. She's tried to help us with all her mother's friends, but she was married ten or so years ago and has lived in the States ever since; she really hasn't been any help. She's taken herself off to Oxford and is staying in the hotel there . . . she'll be off back after the inquest, we expect."

"Has she expressed any desire to see me?"

130

"None at all, sir." Buzz looked crestfallen, even though he did not feel it; it is always slightly depressing to hear people don't want to see you.

"Between ourselves I wouldn't lose any sleep over that."

Running his finger uncomfortably around the inside of his collar, Buzz asked if the daughter was like her mother.

The chief inspector nodded gravely. He lowered his voice and said confidentially: "She knows the lot."

"Oh, good," Buzz returned blandly; "then she will know who killed her mother."

"She thinks she does. . . ."

"Really?"

He had been continuing his work, but now he stopped and looked the chief inspector straight in the face, raising his chin slightly more than he would have wished in order to do so.

The chief inspector's face wore a curious expression as he said nothing.

"Go on . . ." Buzz urged. "Tell me who she thinks dunnit."

"You, Brigadier. . . ."

Buzz turned away, sick. "I see; well, no wonder she doesn't want to meet me."

"We were very severely reprimanded, in fact, for letting you slip through our fingers. But are you not going to tell me the result of your 'wonderings'?"

"I can't help thinking, Chief Inspector, that there is some connection between the murder of Mrs. Furnish and the disappearance of my son. But I find it absolutely impossible to think what the connection could be. Unless Mrs. Gruntz (frightful name) has abducted Joshua."

The chief inspector gave a loud belly laugh, which he instantly suppressed. "It's not funny, of course, I apologize, Brigadier, but as a matter of fact, sir, she has no children of her own and one day she saw Joshua arriving with his brother and your lady help and her son. They all came into the greenhouse just when we happened to be here with her, going around the place once again, you know . . . abduction, eh? It's not too impossible."

"It need not necessarily have been an abduction," Buzz

said carefully. "I am no favorite with Joshua, I regret to say. I could even see Joshua telling her that I had killed her mother. . . ." He looked across at James, who was listening acutely.

"He *could*," James said promptly, "but he didn't. Josh and I do everything together, nearly, and he didn't."

"But you don't always," Buzz pointed out. "You weren't doing things together last Saturday night . . . if you had been he wouldn't have gone, Jimmy. You were with Mr. O'Duff, and Joshua . . . he could have been up to anything on his own, absolutely anything, including hopping off to Oxford and having a long heart-to-heart talk. . . . 'I don't like it at home, Mrs. Gruntz. My father shot your mother for sure, and I shouldn't be there at home.' And she would say: 'Don't go back, come to the States with me. I've got a lovely swimming pool, a fridge with raspberry and chocolate ice cream which pops out when you press a button, hot doughnuts, too. . . !'"

"Stop, stop . . ." James shouted. He started to cry.

Buzz looked at his son out of the well of unhappiness in which he was drowning. "Sorry, really sorry, James."

The chief inspector gazed at the brigadier with something like admiration. He said to James: "But your father could be right. You know, I think everybody knows she's gone to Oxford, and she's staying at the Randolph; where else would a rich American stay? She's told us many a time we could find her there. And boys of Joshua's age do run away; they've been tempted by lesser things than a fridge which spouts ice cream and warm doughnuts, too." There was a half-smile on his face when he said: "We are investigating every possibility and impossibility, and we'll certainly follow up this one, but my guess is he didn't go to Oxford and frat with Mrs. Gruntz."

Both Buzz and James looked questioningly at the CI. Both, of course, wanted that to be the relatively simple explanation, but he shook his head. "It's not for me to describe her, but I do base my belief upon observation."

James turned to his father. "I know what he means; Mrs. Gruntz is just like her mother."

Sick at heart, Buzz went back to his work.

"Well, I'll be seeing you at the inquest, Brigadier, if not before; you know how to get in touch with me if you want me . . . don't hesitate. I do wish you good luck, sir, you do deserve it, if I may say so. And any more ideas you get, sir, give us a tinkle immediately; I have a great admiration for your imagination, if I may say so, sir. It wasn't at all a bad idea of yours, that one, not at all."

A long time after he had gone, when they had nearly finished and were doing some final watering with the hose, James said that it did not look as though the chief inspector thought his father had shot old Ma Furnish; it looked as though it were the very last idea the inspector had in his head. Buzz said that one couldn't be sure; men had been hanged on far fewer fingerprints than he, Buzz, had left about, far less evidence and even less motive.

"Perhaps it's part of the game," he said, "to allow me to think there's no suspicion attached to me, on the old principle of giving me enough rope and I'll hang myself."

When they went back to the pickup the police car had gone, but there was another small car there, into which a young man was packing photographic equipment. "They wanted another photo taken . . ." he explained.

James was already in the pickup when the brigadier asked if he might go into the drawing room and "have a quick look." The young man stated that it was "all the same to him," so James sat and waited the few minutes till the brigadier returned. And when he did, he was smiling very slightly. James asked no questions but he made a mental note of it and was heartened.

After Cart had left for, as always, a destination unknown, Mr. O'Duff dozed in his chair till morning, then trudged heavily up to the attic and woke Joshua, asleep on the dusty floor. He brought him downstairs to the kitchen.

"But, Mr. O'Duff, why can't I go home?"

Mr. O'Duff looked sadly at him. "Joshua," he said, "I have a great respect for your intelligence, great respect."

He peeled a long thick slice of waxy bacon off the main supply, cut it in half and put it in the frying pan. He sliced some cold potato, too, and put it in with the bacon. He did it slowly because there was less than no hurry. They used to give men in the condemned cell a good supper before they topped them next morning, so there was nothing too madly eccentric in his movements now. He liked the child, and he felt sulky and rebellious about having to shoot him, but a duty is a duty, and if you had any sense, you didn't stop to think any more than he had stopped to think about shooting old Ma Furnish. But dammit. . . .

He sulkily swung the egg against the side of the frying pan, thereby breaking the yolk in addition to the shell. "Look at that, now! Carelessness!" He clicked his tongue.

"I don't mind it broken, Mr. O'Duff," Joshua piped (winningly, alas, winningly!). Mr. O'Duff's restless eyes would not stay on Joshua; he avoided looking anywhere other than at the frying pan and its contents as he filled the plate he had been warming for Joshua.

"I was hungry. I had no supper last night, thank you," Joshua said appreciatively when he had finished.

"Now tell me what happened last night."

Joshua looked down, slightly sulky because he felt he had made a fool of himself, been irresponsible and childish, climbing all over the place, breaking windows, just for the fun of the chase.

"You don't know, oh, well, you *do* know, sorry, but it was so exciting waiting for the bird to come, waiting, waiting . . . I . . . well, I was stupid you'll say, I thought I saw it trying to get in a little hole in the top window in the roof. . . ."

"That was it!"

"It was like I was going to lose it and the clock going on and going on, and no pigeon." Crestfallen, when asked, Joshua said he didn't know how it happened, it sounded so silly now, but when he was alone last night in the loft with the clock and ". . . well . . ." he mumbled, head hanging, "I'm too young for all that responsibility. . . ."

Mr. O'Duff took out an extremely dirty handkerchief and wiped his brow. "I don't know about being too young," he gasped. "I'm too old, too old for this kind of thing."

"What kind of thing?" Joshua only half looked up.

When there was no answer, he complained about Cart.

134

"Why was your brother so angry when he found me? What was he doing suddenly coming back, like that, and so terribly, terribly angry?"

"He comes and he goes; he keeps things here, this is his headquarters here in England, he lives in Ireland, and he . . . well, just keeps things here he may need."

"Guns?"

Mr. O'Duff's second-best gun, the Colt Commander .45, was in the kitchen-table drawer with the cooking tools, eight inches or so from his hands as he sat watching Joshua have his meal (the best gun being, it will be remembered, in the Thames River). It was all ready to be used. All he had to do was to pick it up and fire. He opened the drawer wide enough to get it out; the contents of the drawer were just below Joshua's line of vision. Mr. O'Duff put his hand on the rough grip; it felt just like his carrot grater alongside which it lay. Dear God! What a terrible mistake it was to stop and think. Thinking never did anybody any good, as his father had often said: "You know what your aims are? Then don't spend any time thinking about them. Act, take my word for it, *act!*" How right the old man was! To think was to get soggy in the middle. Strong men of action do not stop to think. Stop to think and you're out and outdone!

Joshua leaned over and remarked: "That's a nice revolver, may I look at it?" Mr. O'Duff slammed the drawer shut.

"I say, Mr. O'Duff, you *have* got a lot of guns! Are there nothing but guns in all those boxes stored all over the house?" he asked delightedly.

"No."

"You mean they're something else: gunpowder? Gelignite? I say, Mr. O'Duff, are you a poor man's Guy Fawkes? We've just been learning about him at school: 'Penny for the poor old guy!'" Joshua shrieked with laughter at his own nonjoke.

Mr. O'Duff's face altered, his mouth shriveled to absurdly small proportions, his eyes stared at Joshua from walnut-juice-brown-caves, but Joshua knew when to come in out of the wet. He shuddered slightly, however, as he went on conversationally: "Have you any nail bombs?

They're great, I saw a close-up of one on telly; they don't look anything, but the damage they can do, wow!"

If Cart were to return now, he, Mr. O'Duff, would not answer for either of their lives more than four minutes in his presence. Not that Cart would actually shoot, that had always been against his principles, holy man that he was, but he'd make him shoot Joshua and then himself in shame as a penance. He would cause him to feel, as indeed he already felt, such a deep guilt for betraying the Cause and allowing this kid, with all his guilty knowledge, to live a couple more minutes longer than he should, that he, Con, would immediately remove himself from the world, for betrayal of the greatest cause since the trouble in the Garden of Eden.

"Active service unit number nought, nought, nought," Cart called him with amusement (not with laughter; Cart never laughed).

And now Mr. O'Duff was writhing, squirming with sheer embarrassment in his chair, Joshua's piping voice grinding into him like a power drill. "If I can help you, me and James, with the Fancy, why can't we help you with the IRA?"

He wasn't a normal child; he was a monster! Mr. O'Duff was outraged; he felt stripped of not only his clothes, but his flesh, and was sitting in his bones shuddering in his kitchen chair.

"Are you ill, Mr. O'Duff?"

He had read in some Sunday paper or other that children developed early these days, but this! He said: "It bangs bannacker!"

"What, Mr. O'Duff?"

He got up and staggered stiffly to the sink, carrying the kettle, and pouring out some hot water, he started to wash up the dishes left from Joshua's meal. Though the house was air-conditioned, there was no hot-water system, so for the ten years of his habitation Mr. O'Duff had never had a bath; one week he would, as he had told the boys, "wash up as far as possible" and the next week "wash down as far as possible," and all this in the same sink over which he now crouched, unnerved. "Cleanliness," he had told the boys, "is next to godliness," and Joshua now sprang up willingly, clutching the unspeakably dirty tea towel, or piece of old sheet, and dried the dishes.

Here in this child was an embryo gem for anarchy; there is no doubt that anarchists were short on the brains side; in another ten years Joshua could be God's gift to anarchy. Guerrilla squads properly organized were even more important than racing pigeons, which, after all, were a hobby, a hobby as distinct from a campaign.

"Joshua, I am going to lock you up in the lockup."

"Where's that?"

"It's down the cellar. . . ."

"I've never seen it."

"Nor had you seen anything else in this house except in my quarters until last night."

"What is it, Mr. O'Duff?"

"We had it constructed a long time ago in the event of an emergency. The need to lock someone up, we'll say. It's clean and tidy and comfortable, and there's a radio in it. I'm going to keep you down there, boy, till this has all blown over."

"This what, Mr. O'Duff?"

"Until after May fourteenth, Josh boy."

"What's that, St. Carthage's birthday?"

"And me brother's birthday. After that. . . ."

"Oh, do explain, Mr. O'Duff"—Joshua was becoming exasperated—"go on, go on. . . ."

"Me brother Cart, Joshua, he's a kind of man, only a kind, I say . . . he's an extremist, he wouldn't kill anybody, mind, never do that, but he'd well . . . see they was destroyed if they was interfering with his . . . his ambitions. He's a lovely man out there in the loft, talking about the Fancy, but, Joshua, I *know* he's the divil himself if. . . ."

"If what, Mr. O'Duff?"

"If his plans are going wrong. He's a marvelous man, mark you. . . ."

"So you're going to lock me up in the cellar whilst he's here?"

Mr. O'Duff started visibly. "More than that, I can't be sure when he will be here, he's organizing this big . . . well,

I never know . . . as I say, he comes and he goes, but if he comes and finds you still around. . . ."

Joshua's face crumpled; it was almost as though he were about to cry, but powers within were having an effect upon him. Fascinated, Mr. O'Duff watched the expressions crossing his face; would he, or would he not, cry? It was as though the boy had seen the meaning behind Mr. O'Duff's evasions and clumsy pseudoexplanations.

"We don't want no trouble," Mr. O'Duff countered invidiously. "And I can't do widdout you, Joshua boy, and that's a fack! I rely on you to . . . to do all the necessary in the loft when I . . . when I'm absent. I never had a helper like you and your brother. Reliable . . ." he put in quickly but weakly, "except for last night. On the whole, yes. Good boys. So I must look after you, Joshua, protect you from . . . from, er. . . ."

"Oh, it's all right," Joshua said impatiently, "you can cut the cackle, I'll come quietly."

Those four cellar windows in the front of the house, two on either side of the front door, standing on tiptoe to see out, closely shuttered, were storerooms similar to the others, all of them air-conditioned because, essential as it was to store explosives in an even temperature, free from damp, the cellar was the dampest place of the lot. It had cost a great deal to install this air conditioning; after the initial cost of the house, almost the whole of the rest of the small fortune that O'Duff senior had left to his sons had gone on that. Con had been left half, and Carthage had been left the other half. And O'Duff father, being a just man and knowing that his other children were making a living, he left his money to the son who had helped him so ably with the business and also to the one who was God's champion upon earth, in equal halves (thereby, possibly, doing himself a good turn in that direction).

Thus the two men were joint owners of the house, and peace and comfort such as are enjoyed by the majority having no attraction for either of them, they spent the money for the Cause. They hadn't known what to do with the small windowless cellar room in the middle of the house, 7 feet by 11 feet. Though it had been air-conditioned like the rest, it had remained unused since inauguration, with the same locking system on the doors as existed everywhere else. It would come in useful, perhaps someday, was the general opinion.

Never having experienced being locked up in his life, Joshua helped Mr. O'Duff prepare for his imprisonment with enthusiasm and shining eyes. "There's that old flea bag of yours I could sleep in!" he exclaimed in excited anticipation. "I'll sleep on the floor!"

But that was going too far. Mr. O'Duff insisted that they drag down the cellar steps one of the three flimsy mattresses from Mr. O'Duff's own bed. They carried down a foot-high bundle of the *Racing Pigeon*, and Mr. O'Duff fixed up a new bulb in the flex hanging from the center of the ceiling. An old oak milking stool, a tin of macaroons (given Mr. O'Duff some five years ago at Christmas by a lady admirer, but unopened because Mr. O'Duff did not like macaroons: something to do with his teeth), a pencil and an old writing-pad for making notes, a draftboard and men, a weather-beaten pack of cards, a potty and roll of paper, a radio set. In the excitement of the preparations Mr. O'Duff shed his cares; his face grew to its normal proportions, becoming less shriveled. As a final treat he brought down *Foxe's Book of Martyrs* which he had sometimes shown them on a wet afternoon, telling Joshua to take great care of it; it was a family heirloom. They looked around, wondering how they could add to his future comfort, and remembered that a large bottle of water might be useful. Somewhere in the depths of that kitchen dresser there was one of those straw-covered pitchers, brought from Spain a very long time ago, and after a good rinsing it was filled with water and carried down to what Joshua delightedly called his "pad."

Finally he sat down in the center of the mattress, wrapped his arms around his knees and said: "Maggie's going to miss me!"

"Ah, you rascal!" Mr. O'Duff cried, carried away by the fun of it all. "You want me to go and fetch that tiny hound! I'll not do that, the poor wee thing! I'll be seeing you, Josh, boy; I'll keep you posted; if you want anything, just call. Bye-bye, then!" He waved, looking back through the space left before he finally shut the door, and winking, he locked the padlock.

Joshua did want something, which he remembered before Mr. O'Duff could have traveled more than twenty feet away and started to climb the stairs; it was a gun, all part of the game.

"Mr. O'Duff!" he shouted. "Please can I have one of your guns?"

No answer, because Mr. O'Duff did not hear. It was not that the little dungeon had been soundproofed, but simply that the house had been built three hundred years ago and the foundations dated back much farther than the brick residence constructed above it.

After he had shouted his name half a dozen times Joshua's voice had risen to a scream, but the drop from having fun to becoming hysterical was not necessarily so rapid; he became thoughtful, wondering. So he could not be heard? Or Mr. O'Duff did not want to hear? Oh, he heard all right, but for reasons of his own did not wish to return to find out what he wanted?

Joshua picked up one of the magazines and idly turned the pages: pigeons, pigeons, pigeons, all exactly the same except for the direction in which they were looking, left or right. Only not to an expert, and Joshua was now an expert. He became engrossed and presently needed scissors to cut out photographs of one or two beauties to pin up on his bedroom wall. "Scissors!" he yelled. "Scissors!" he screamed. "SCISSORS!"

16

Still mildly elated, Mr. O'Duff returned to the kitchen and banged the kettle on. He was very thoughtful, so much so that he did not empty the teapot and put in fresh leaves, but when the kettle boiled, he poured the water upon the old tea leaves from breakfast and started sipping the brown-purple brew that he poured out. May 10 the calendar read; he sedulously tore off the date every morning. There were four days to go. Cart had not said for sure whether he would come or not for the big operation. On the night of the fourteenth/fifteenth the old house was to be cleared from attics to cellars of ammunition: revolvers, bullets and holsters (because revolvers were the best for guerrilla fighting in the main), but there were ninety rifles, a great deal of nitroglycerine and many component parts required in the making of bombs by amateurs using the kitchen sink. Nitroglycerine is a nuisance to lug about because it is ultrasensitive and may explode if dropped or nudged too roughly.

There had been operations similar to the one proposed and successfully carried out for the past five years; so far there had been no accident, but it all seemed to rest upon the capable shoulders of Mr. O'Duff's brother Cart. Mr. O'Duff was dumb, literally, with admiration for Cart; his efficiency was remarkable. Small trucks came for the firearms, but the explosives were carried in what they referred to as "luxury" vans; last time a fleet of no less than eleven of them had carried off the "delicacies," as Mr. O'Duff called them. On three out of the five occasions Cart had been there part of the time, waiting until the operation was successfully under way and leaving before it was over to call at the approved stopping places on the way to the west coast, checking upon the drivers. There was little doubt that during the operations Cart was under great strain; he ate and drank nothing and had an unpleasant habit of referring to these approved stops as the "stations of the cross."

Then for weeks the house would be empty; Mr. O'Duff would walk around his empty mansion from time to time with a marvelous sense of power and freedom, all the responsibility relegated, until the restocking started.

Mr. O'Duff had his doubts about the big job, as they called it; he, personally, would like the materials to go out as quickly as they came in, a smart turnover he called it in discussions with Cart. But alas, everything hung on the weather and the roughness of seas. The weather in the Irish Channel was more often than not unspeakable and sick-making. It could almost never be relied upon, even in the three months of midsummer. But on the other hand the chances were better in these three months, and the vehicles wasted less time waiting around for calm seas. Time cost money, and as there was by no means unlimited money, there had to be a date for the big collection. The vehicles went to any and every port available for maritime transport and sailed when the sea was calm, which might be at once or might be in a week's time, at the worst.

Four days to go.

Cart thought of everything. "Don't have those damn kids around so much," he warned. "Sooner or later they'll start to wonder, things being delivered so often . . . of course they'll wonder."

"I make out it's me pigeon food!"

"There's a limit to the amount pigeons can eat," Cart sneered coldly. "Send them packing," he had said, "I'm telling you. Get rid of them; no good will come of it having them around."

That had been when they first came to the lodge, and a great deal of tact, gentle persuasion and sheer grinding persistence had gone into gently rolling out Cart's obsession about the kids. Only recently he had brought it up again. As D day approached, he had once more become querulous about the boys, and this had once again been slid over by the construction of the barrel loft, with much grunting and cursing, which took the boys away into the paddock for a lot of time. It was only a makeshift remedy, but it had appeased for the time being.

Getting the better of Cart was no mean achievement, and how long could it go on? Cart was in a different mental category altogether from his brother Con; monastery-educated, Cart's brain had developed. Con's brain was a small shriveled thing in his head of which he was ashamed, because it didn't work except in small bursts, like a faulty lawn mower.

Mr. O'Duff poured himself another cup of tea and

sighed heavily; he felt so rotten. He knew it was bad for him to drink so much strong tea and to eat so little. He had been told by an imaginative doctor that the lining of his stomach was like a piece of dried leather, tannic-treated to the pitch when it would make a pair of snow shoes, and that was why he had the stomach pains which were the killing of him. That, this doctor had said, and the constant anxiety state in which he lived . . . but this last Mr. O'Duff denied vigorously; what did that whippersnapper know about his state of mind, even if he was sharp about his stomach? He never went to him again.

What reason might Cart have for coming back before D day? Who could possibly foretell what emergency would bring him back? If Joshua could remain concealed until after the big event on the fourteenth/fifteenth, it was possible, *just* possible that if the operation had gone smoothly as before, Cart would be sublimely relaxed and tolerant; it had happened like that at least twice. When everything had gone without the smallest hitch, Cart would turn up, glowing with the love of God, peace on earth and goodwill to all mankind (except those invaders, still living upon the Holy Soil of Ireland, of course), and a little child could play with him then. He would be so blinded by success that he would look at Joshua without remembering, maybe, that he should not be visible but have been shot dead early in May.

On the other hand, if Mr. O'Duff could succeed in bringing off his fearful deception and avoid shooting Joshua, as instructed, until after D day, Mr. O'Duff himself could play it cunning. He could have a private talk with the brigadier, a sound man Mr. O'Duff considered him, and a man to be trusted—he could have this talk and advise him either to send his son away to a boarding school and keep him hidden during the holidays or, better still, move away from the district altogether.

The brigadier would want to know the reason for this advice, but he would just have to go on wanting, that was all.

What a hellish mess! With one hand holding up his heavy head, exhausted with thinking, Mr. O'Duff opened the kitchen drawer and brought out the revolver. He stared at it. Perhaps his thoughts had been a lot of fancy stuff; perhaps much the best thing was to creep into the cellar in the early hours, when Joshua was at his deepest sleep, and finish off the job.

Joshua was too bright, much too bright a child to have around in the dicey circumstances; television-conditioned, he knew everything there was to know about anarchy, revolutions and explosives; he would know by sight most of the revolutionaries who had erupted into the public eye in the last year or so; he would understand what the O'Duff brothers were about, and he was a soldier's son who knew what soldiers were for. The whole damned Joshua thing was hopeless. Hopeless. Mr. O'Duff lowered his head upon his arms, folded on the table, and he still held the revolver. He had never cried, he didn't know how; tears had never fallen from those tiny boot buttons deep in the walnut-brown hollows where eyes usually were.

He was, in his own way, weeping great heartbroken sobs for the boy in the dungeon; not that he loved him, because he did not have the machinery for any kind of love. And yet, and yet, if anyone had asked him if he would sacrifice his beliefs to save the boy's life, he would have chosen to toss away that young life without any hesitation and to continue his campaign to destroy the invader upon the Holy Soil of Ireland every time.

The okay word for which his mind had been groping for some time came suddenly to him next morning as he was scraping out the food bucket from the pigeon loft: "indoctrinate," a lovely brainy word which he kept rolling around his mouth like a humbug. With this fine clever word he might be forgiven for failing in his duty to the Cause. Because he had to admit that in spite of the good clean idea he had had about the disposal of the body, he found himself as little able to perform the act as he would be to stand on his head on the kitchen table. The will was there, he told himself, but he lacked the ability, an excellent shot like himself; he was ashamed. Ashamed on two counts, that he lacked the will to shoot the boy at all, and secondly, he lacked the ability to grab hold of his gun and damned well do it. If

144

things were left as they were, he would be condemned by all right-thinking people as a shocking renegade.

Renegade! The finger of derision would be pointed at him notwithstanding all the dangerous work he had already done for the Cause. Opinion changed so quickly; folks were so bitterly ready to scorn and reject. So surely, to *indoctrinate* his prisoner would be to put himself in the right with everyone concerned, including the Holy Saints.

He sliced some cold potato; he peeled a thick slice of bacon from the main bulk, as he did and had done about twice a day for thirty years. He ate his own meal first, then prepared another the same and took it down to Joshua on a tray, together with a steaming mug of tea so strong you could stand the spoon upright in it, nearly.

The boy seemed strangely depressed, lying on the mattress, the sleeping bag pushed to one side.

"The top o' the morning to yez!"

"Is it morning? What day is it?"

"It's Tuesday the eleventh of May."

"Father will be coming home," Joshua said as he addressed himself to his meal, legs crossed with the tray on the mattress in front of him. "Mrs. Flower will have sent for him. The police will be looking for 'the missing boy' . . . that's me."

Squatting on the floor opposite, Con watched him with hand across the lower half of his face, eyes darting about. That the police had been here already was not significant; he was on excellent terms with them, and they were reassured of the thoroughness of his search in the house. He had made a variety of suggestions where the missing boy could be and had even spent an hour with them beating the bounds for signs of him. He had given it as his considered opinion that Joshua, having somehow come by some money, had gone to the great metropolis to seek his fortune. Which great metropolis? Con spread his hands wide, meaning that it was anybody's guess. Every boy, he had told them as from his deep well of experience, every boy at some time in his development wanted to leave home and go it on his own.

In ten years nobody had appeared ever to voice curiosity

145

about the shuttered house. Because Mr. O'Duff was a devotee of the Fancy, it was taken for granted that he had bought the house for the stables which converted easily into an excellent pigeon loft of the first class. Even when, one day, a group of people had called seeking houses worthy of preservation orders, they had been perfectly amiable toward Mr. O'Duff's embarrassed apologies about not showing them over the house. Art treasures, he explained, were being stored for a business friend in the art world, and the rooms had to be kept carefully closed to preserve an even temperature. One day hot, one day icy cold, he complained, it was a source of constant anxiety to him. They considered this perfectly reasonable. Nobody could be more reasonable than Mr. O'Duff when he was being reasonable, and vice versa.

He started the—what was it?—*indoctrination,* dammit, he'd forgotten the word already; it was oily and unattractive to start with anyway. "How would you feel if a lot of wild men came from over the seas and took a part of your country off you, smashing your images, standing on your faces . . ." and so on.

Joshua frowned. "Images; what images?"

Mr. O'Duff frowned too, it was difficult to explain. "Your treasures," he tried vaguely, "everything you found . . . well, what shall we call it? Oh, boy! you must know what treasures are!"

But Joshua was not only with him; he was way ahead and dragging him along behind. "I'd shoot them dead, I'd bash them, I'd chase them away. . . ." Replenished by his meal, he gave an energetic demonstration of how he could behave, standing up on the mattress and lashing out to right and to left with a supposedly hideously frightening face.

Mr. O'Duff had reckoned on this "indoctrination" taking three days, from now till May 14/15. The more he thought about it, the more sure he was that Cart would come; it would all depend upon the qualities of his drivers. If he felt they were all totally dependable, he might not come. But if he found he was employing any clumsy, stupid oafs, he would have to be here and watch the loading of every single vehicle. Of course Con hoped passionately, prayed, that Cart would not find out that Joshua was still alive, and he intended thoroughly to reassure Cart as to the disposal of the body (not, in this particular case, the box plan). But Cart was so cruelly clever that his brother did not for one moment really believe he was going to get away with it.

So in the last resort, he would have to cry: "Yes, yes, Joshua is still alive, Cart, but"—and then this difficult word—"indoctrinated and a lifelong Sinn Feiner."

By that time the word would have flown back to his memory like a homing pigeon, and he would have trapped it by writing it down on the kitchen slate with the piece of chalk he used when he needed to remind himself what he needed at the shops.

In actual fact Mr. O'Duff had not the slightest idea what he would do when the time to May 14 was up, and even unknown to himself, he was relying on the uncertainty of his brother returning. The pipedream was that Cart would be transported with delight that the captive boy had been—that was it! *indoctrinated*—and would take him away with him to see the arms and ammunition safely at their place of destination.

Now he found that it had taken less than four minutes to indoctrinate Joshua . . . he was thrown. It would have to be the gun after all.

17

Missing boy or no missing boy, Mrs. Flower "knew her place" (an anachronism she had learned when young from her mother who had been "in service") and on the day that the brigadier should have returned (and did) in answer to her telegram, she folded up her camp bed, packed her fiber case and prepared to return to her own home. But her anxiety was such that she had little sleep, cycling madly home about eleven o'clock and back at the lodge by 9 A.M.

She flew to the window with every vehicle that passed and rushed hopefully to answer the telephone every time it rang. Tea and sympathy were constantly available; she lost weight. The brigadier did not lose weight, but after a week with her he lost hope; he moved about stiffly as one in a nightmare, sleepwalking, and he ate mindlessly. Mrs. Flower told herself she could well serve up a boiled dishcloth and he would eat it. When she went into his bedroom with the vacuum cleaner, she noted with grief that far from sleeping, the brigadier did not even lie upon his bed, which retained the dent made by Maggie exactly. She told herself that he was "living on his nerves" and that it could only end in his having a breakdown, but there was nothing she could do but stick it and support him silently and steadily.

The inquest reopened without any surprises; as chief deponent the brigadier gave his evidence curtly and unemotionally, going through the whole story which had now become stale, word for word as he had gone through it before. He was aware of the hard stare across the court of the woman who was unmistakably the daughter of Mrs. Furnish. Predictably she would be certain he was guilty and had employed a barrister on her own account, who put questions to him intended to draw the attention of the coroner to the obvious guilt of the brigadier. This was not successful, however, being far too evident. But had he been guilty, they might well have caused the witness to break down and confess all, there and then.

The coroner had been obliged to summon a jury and in his final address directed them as to the verdict, which was, of course, murder charging the redoubtable person or persons unknown. Buzz walked out of the court quickly, knowing that Mrs. Gruntz was after him, climbed into his pickup, which was now behaving admirably, and sped away. The death of Mrs. Furnish was her problem, not his. He had enough on his plate.

Alone in the sitting room, tea beside him and sympathy

positively oozing through the wall, he took out his notecase and extracted from it the check given him in Janhara, and signed in Arabic.

He had been amused at their endorsement of it for cash, picturing himself staggering away from the bank, down Piccadilly, with a bag of gold. It was an absurd amount of money, he thought, but then, the money received in royalties by the sheikhs of the states concerned in the oil rush had always seemed to him, somehow, unreal. That a sheikh could leave his Claridge's suite for a shopping "spree" and return an hour or so later having bought three Rolls-Royces and a Range Rover for local use had always struck him as laughable.

As he held it between his fingers, it meant nothing to him; at the time of receiving it he had had some pleasure in thinking about the ease with which he would pay the fees for James and Joshua at the best school he could find at which they had two vacancies. He thought then about the greenhouse he would build, portable because of the possibility of their moving from their rented house. But there was no longer any pleasure in these thoughts, without Joshua.

What did happen, though, was the idea that Joshua could possibly be returned to him in exchange for this slip of paper.

Why did he not think of it before . . . a reward offered?

He telephoned to the chief inspector's office, asking him to come and see him as soon as possible.

He told Mrs. Flower that it was getting on for the day on which he should properly have returned from his trip; his mother would be expecting news of him. In view of the horrible facts he had to apprize her of, he intended to go to London tomorrow to see her and to the Foreign Office with all the details of his trip, written out and ready to deliver in his dispatch case.

He sat and waited for the chief inspector, who came in such spare time as he had, after his evening meal, when James had been sent to bed.

"I'm not wholly in favor, Brigadier," he said deflatingly

when the idea had been revealed. *"Reward Offered* is uninspiring these days. It would have to be one whale of a reward. . . ." He looked at him sadly.

"But it is!" Buzz cried.

He could not bring himself to state the sum on the check; it was honestly and simply a tip, quite apart from and in addition to the fee he would receive from the FO for services rendered. To be tipped this vast sum of money was beyond credibility to anybody who did not know the situation thoroughly.

"Four figures?" the chief inspector put in tentatively.

"Yes . . ." Buzz returned almost in a whisper, hating every moment of it.

The chief inspector murmured thoughtfully: "A thousand pounds in cash for the return of your son . . . we can try it, if you like."

But later, when he had gone, Buzz beat his temples with his two wrists; he had, in spite of all that was at stake, been too cowardly to come out with the precise sum. He must talk over the idea of a reward with someone, and in the absence of a friend he thought of his nearest neighbor, though he had already talked enough with Mr. O'Duff about Joshua. He had been kindly and understanding up to a point, but he had completely failed to come out with any ideas about where he was, other than an often-repeated "But, Brigadier, sorr, you're one of many mourning fathers whose young boys have left home. . . ." True, he used as many varieties of this explanation as he could think of, but in the end they came to the same thing. He would harp on the old Victorian thing of boys running away to sea, which made Buzz grind his teeth.

However, he hurried up the drive not long after nine, with Maggie at his heels, when the blackbirds were fluting away in the rhododendrons. He wanted to test Mr. O'Duff's reaction to the offer of an enormous cash reward for producing information which would lead to the restoration to him of his son. Not that he thought for a moment Mr. O'Duff had the slightest idea where Joshua was, but he might give Buzz some idea how the man in the street, who might possibly know something, would feel about this mooted cash reward.

Mr. O'Duff received them somewhat breathlessly, explaining that he had carried the barrel of porter into his pantry and his breathing wasn't as good as it had been. He tapped his chest in an explanatory gesture and looked down with dislike at Maggie. He had shut the door behind him and was not going to ask the brigadier in.

Buzz then said that he wanted a little talk with him and this time he was not going to do it standing in the yard. "Shall we?" He moved his head in the direction of the back door, clearly indicating that he would like to go in. He intended to bring out the check from Janhara, in order to add verisimilitude and corroborative detail to his otherwise unconvincing narrative, etc.

"I can't let you in, sorr, I'm not too clean in me habits; the kitchen is in a fine state this day—it's the birds keep me at it; keeping them clean is enough for any man." Mr. O'Duff giggled out his long excuse. There was a broken-down garden seat among the weeds in the front drive. He led them there and sat down, saying: "What have you got to show me then, this lovely evening?"

Buzz pulled it out of his pocket like the legendary conjuror. "How would this affect the kidnapper of Joshua . . . in cash, think you?"

Curiously . . . there was no doubt about it. Mr. O'Duff seemed completely turned to stone and for so long that Buzz half turned to look at him. He had always a dark, dark face, but now it was become even darker, or was it the early summer twilight, rapidly failing into dark?

He seemed to be trying to speak, but it was a long time before anything sensible came out of his mouth, preceded by a lot of throat clearings.

"To be quite honest, Brigadier, to be quite honest. . . ."

"Yes?"

"There's no doubt at all, he would send the boy back home pretty quick."

"There would be the old difficulty about handing over the cash, with the police waiting in disguise to catch the kidnapper. . . ."

"If he *had* kidnapped the boy. But how would the notice of the reward go: would it be . . . 'to anyone returning' . . . or would it be . . . 'to anyone offering information.' . . . You've got to decide."

"That would depend upon the circumstances, of course."

Hideously, Mr. O'Duff started to make a strange sound. "There's only one way I can think of you could do it, provided it *was* someone kidnapped him, or, or *was* keeping him for some foul purposes of his own, like . . . he'd have to collect it by helicopter, hee-hee-hee!" It wasn't normal laughter; Mr. O'Duff, who never laughed, was convulsed. He was doubled up, and were there an aisle to roll in, he would have been rolling in the aisle.

Buzz stirred restlessly upon the seat beside him, and Maggie raised her head and looked at him anxiously; of course he knew the man was slightly mad, but he had given much pleasure and amusement to his boys—he must be stood if not understood. The near laughter made him uncomfortable; he had never heard Mr. O'Duff laugh that he could remember. It was a strange, cobweb-hung noise that had clearly not been used for many years, if ever. Perhaps he was having some kind of minor fit, a *petit mal* as the French call it.

"I suppose it is an absurdly far-fetched notion, kidnapping," Buzz mused aloud, "but. . . ." What he was trying to say was more difficult than it might have been if he were not able to put it into words which he himself understood, but it was based upon the successful job he had completed in Janhara. In all his years of employment in the Middle East he had never been threatened or molested, but now . . . he wondered, everyone was everywhere. On the broken-down seat beside the giggling Irishman in the lovely birdsong of the late spring evening he now admitted to himself that Sherbia *could have* been followed down here into the shires, the lodge *could have* been under observation, and in order that pressure could be put one way or another upon this henchman of the sheikh, his son *could have* been, what? Abducted . . . kidnapped . . . garroted (no, that was

152

Spanish, he was being fanciful) . . . held in captivity was more like it.

Uncannily Mr. O'Duff seemed to be following his train of thought.

"You have some very strange folk come around from time to time, it would seem," he leered, remembering the visitation of the Cadillac and its passengers. "Those who get themselves mixed up in those wicked goings-on out there in the Holy Land should expect trouble, but I would not have thought kidnapping a child would come into it. I don't want to say it, sorr, but sudden death would seem to me more like it . . ." but he could not take his eyes off the check at which he stared with popping eyes of, almost, fear, and he held his twitching hands firmly together. "Hands off Jerusalem, is what I would say," he advised, but almost absently as though he were thinking of something else, which he was. "I wouldn't touch a job to do with that Holy City meself . . ." and he even went so far as to sign himself with the cross superstitiously. But now he was longing for his visitor to leave, he had a frightful headache across his forehead; he wanted to be alone to sort out his new, new thoughts because the great aching misery of it was, if Joshua was *not* to be painlessly put away, to be as it were exchanged for this check, what was to happen to the boy? Was he to be adopted and drawn into the group as one of them?

It was too utterly unrealistic to imagine such a thing; it might happen in books, but in real life Joshua was one great big headache.

Mrs. Furnish, too, had been a headache for the few hours until he had shot her, and he hadn't hesitated much longer than it took to load the gun to do that.

Why then should he have brought this monstrous problem on himself by not being decisive about Joshua? He who hesitates is lost, as his ould mother used to say, and she was always right, God rest her soul. And absolutely like an automaton, he crossed himself again.

Buzz felt the small hairs rising upward along his spine. He leaned forward, elbows on his knees and check still between his two hands. He did not wish to see the chilling behavior of his companion, who took his mind off the problem in hand.

"You're not being helpful, Mr. O'Duff. In fact, I find your behavior rather strange!" And, by God, he did, come to think of it. "I simply came to ask if *you* thought to publish this in, say, the local paper and perhaps a small ad in the *Times* would cause anyone who knew anything *vital* about Joshua's disappearance to go to the police or come to me or. . . ."

"Publish what?"

"An advertisement, for want of a better name, stating the amount of the reward offered for information leading to the return of my son. . . ."

Mr. O'Duff cut in: ". . . and it would be the whole amount of this check, the *whole* amount. . . ."

Doubtless, if Mr. O'Duff had been able to conceal the excitement in his voice, he would have done so, or perhaps he was not even aware of it.

Buzz felt he was getting no kind of sense out of the man. He was all expert information and snappy answers on the subject of pigeons, which was the only subject upon which he had conversed with him at length, but about anything else, Buzz now felt, he was useless. That was the impression he gave, anyway.

He stood up to go, and Mr. O'Duff stood up too. Suddenly the standing up brought him back to hard facts. He said: "You can kidnap a baby or a kid up to, say, five, but after that there's endless difficulties, just think of them now! Whoever is returned to their folk will have a long spiel to tell, will they not, now? Joshua has all his buttons on, as they say. How could he be silenced? Think that over, will you?"

A thrush on the old magnolia poured out advice in a long, clear cadenza.

"I tell you, man," Mr. O'Duff croaked, "a bloke could claim the money all right, but he could only live to enjoy it if he returned the captive dead"—pause—"*dead,* I said!"

"I heard you!"

As Buzz stumped away across the gravel Mr. O'Duff

noticed that he was still carrying the check. He was carrying it with the lack of care of someone carrying a dirty floor cloth, by one corner, with the tips of his fingers. Maggie was hurrying after him, clearly forgotten.

"A bloody man!" Buzz fumed.

It would be nice to say that he strode off down the drive in a towering rage, but inaccurate because it is difficult to stride when you are short and fat. He trotted off, but inside was a huge striding warrior, struggling to get out, carrying Mr. O'Duff's severed bleeding head by its thick gray hair.

The telephone was ringing in the lodge. He burst in and picked up the receiver.

It was dear Lucy, his sister-in-law. "Buzz darling, thank you, thank you, thank you! You are a darling, generous *idiot. . . .*" It took him a good minute to bring himself back from outer space where he had suddenly been in receipt of an idea. It wasn't an idea so much as a message, though he didn't believe in extrasensory perception or any of what was now called "jabberwocky" instead of "tommyrot."

It was when that thrush was carrying on from the magnolia; he knew without the slightest doubt that Mr. O'Duff was totally aware of the whole situation regarding Joshua and a lot more besides.

His sister-in-law was thanking him, it seemed, for some rug or carpet or other he seemed to have given her a long time ago. "Are you there, Buzz?" she kept saying. The thing was that it had been held up in the customs and had only arrived today, this afternoon in fact. The customs people had been confirming that it was, indeed, as old as it had to be to avoid import duty.

"Are you there, Buzz?"

But in any case, soon after she had arrived home from the meeting with Buzz in Beirut, she and her husband had to go to Ireland: ". . . about darling Fatty." The police wanted them there for some identification of something that had belonged to their son. She couldn't explain now, but there were great efforts going on there to round up the gang responsible for his death.

And again about the rug: "Do you know, Buzz, I didn't

believe it was mine when I landed in London; in fact, I declared it wasn't, even though my name was on it, and then everybody thought it was a bomb planted in the plane in Beirut, and then finally they found the stewardess who had allowed you to bring it on board as hand luggage, because it was so valuable, you had told her. She must have been impressed by your ER II dispatch case, old dear!" Lucy laughed. "You're very quiet, darling. . . ." She sounded anxious suddenly.

He couldn't, he could not bring himself to tell her about Joshua. She did not have to know, so why worry her until there was reason to rejoice at his return? He answered the "How's everybody?" question gruffly and said, when invited to stay with them in August, they would love to come, and finally they rang off. He was quite aware that when she put down the receiver she would turn to her husband and remark that there was something wrong with Buzz, but it couldn't be helped.

The IRA. The IRA and Mr. O'Duff. The fancier.

Like with receivers of stolen goods, there was always something else; these people with missions, the undergrounders, as it were, they always had an occupation: the spies who were artists, the fence who was a fishmonger, the burglar who was a window cleaner (a cliché that one!), the terrorist a barber: he had heard of many instances but always the miscreant had an occupation slightly offbeat.

Which came first, the well-known fancier or the militant Republican? Of course, it was he who had shot Mrs. Furnish. Buzz knew it without a shadow of doubt; she must have been prying, that afternoon he was in town and the boys back from school and extremely offhand with her, as they could be. She had taken to exploring; she was great at that. Just plain damned curiosity he called it. Not that curiosity was a bad thing, far from it, but it was that kind of curiosity which has assumed a new name . . . snooping. She had been snooping, that afternoon, and in the evening after dinner, back at her home, she had been trying to tell him about her suspicions. And he . . . he had been so absolutely certain she was mischief-making that he had endeavored to shut her up.

And when, after the awful scene in the kitchen, probably observed under the undrawn blinds at the kitchen window, he had left, the observer seeing her alone had gone around to the front, rang the bell.

O'Duff would have already met her that afternoon, perhaps, perhaps. . . .

She would know him by sight, maybe want to talk to him about what she had observed in the afternoon, "up at his place." Mysterious unloadings, perhaps. That was why she opened the door to him so late at night. He was a man she knew by sight, if only slightly. He had come to discuss something with her, so she opened the door to him.

Would it be something to do with the Patricott boys? If so, it was certain that she would not hesitate to let him in.

Or was it something else, associated with his political convictions? That too would cause her to open the door to him; a magistrate, she might often have people calling casually to discuss with her things important to them.

He realized, as the thought flashed through his head and he gave it a curt nod in passing, that he no longer cared who killed Mrs. Furnish, but what was certain was that the man who could shoot her in, as they say, *cold blood* could do the same with Joshua had he been discovered in compromising circumstances, in other words, fiddling with the locks or any other thing.

He went into the kitchen and made himself a strong cup of instant coffee. He stirred in a large spoonful of sugar to revive his shocked brain. Soon he did some practical thinking about stark things like hacksaws and huge slabs of putty or the equivalent, for "breaking and entering."

Hacksaws, in fact, would be irrelevant because of the confounded shutters. Not that he had ever had a chance of seeing any of those shutters up at the house from the inside, but he did remember from his youth, when his mother and father had lived in a little house in the town of Windsor, that that had the same sort of shutters. He had often wondered why they were not made now; they offered luxurious freedom from drafts on cold winter nights and complete security from burglars.

To enter a window was relatively easy, but to enter a shuttered window there has to be a tremendous amount of wood splitting. They fit beautifully, and when opened out, there is seen to be a thin, thin flat iron bar which drops down onto a flat bracket slot and locks the whole shutter tight.

But why enter at all since he thought he *knew* what was inside: implements of war. But since he also knew, because the boys had told him, that Mr. O'Duff's house was air-conditioned, it might follow that ammunition was stored therein: this could mean a number of things: nitrocellulose, nitroglycerine for making blasting gelatine . . . in fact, any and every explosive compound should be kept in good atmospheric conditions, not liable to damp or heat. The worst explosive compound of the lot, TNT, can still be made at home. There might be machine guns and hand grenades galore. They would be harmless without the bang-bang stuff, so it was a safe bet that a "consignment" of arms for the revolutionaries would contain the proper proportions of it.

But how many loads had come and gone from here since their occupation of the lodge? Did they come and go in small lots or at intervals of weeks or months or even years?

Why had he never wondered at the amount of traffic coming and going from the big house? Pigeon food! That was always the answer. It would have been laughable if it hadn't been so deathly unfunny.

18

"James . . . you're not having any breakfast worth mentioning!"

James had lost weight; he was dull-eyed and jumped when spoken to. "I'm not hungry, Father."

"You must eat this egg I've boiled for you, Jamie boy. Sit down again, I want to talk to you. Go on, take the top off while I ask you things."

Sadly and reluctantly James did as he was bidden.

"It's about your friend Mr. O'Duff. I had a long talk with him last night. We sat out on the front seat, that broken thing. He didn't ask me in."

"He never does."

"You mean. . . ."

"We go into his kitchen for hours, but he gets very cross if we start, as he calls it, wandering about. Joshua and I have never been past the green woolly door that swings backwards and forwards from the passage into the hall."

"So he lives entirely in the servants' quarters, eh? Have you ever wondered what he does with the rest of the house?"

James looked up, interested for the first time.

"No, he's often said he picked up the house cheap, because folk were taking their time about buying it; he says he snapped it up, and it's much too big for him."

"I'll say it is."

"But he wanted the stables, you see. He's made this huge loft and all the storage space for food and sand and . . . things."

James finished his egg, turned it upside down and hit it with his spoon until it was reduced to rubble in his eggcup. "What do *you* think he stores there in the house?"

"I think it's an ammunition dump, since you've asked me."

159

James' mouth fell open; it must be said that it fell open easily, but this time there really was something for it to fall open about.

"From cellar to attic, I'd say, jammed with war matériel."

"But he's a pigeon man!" James stammered. "Why . . . why?"

"Yes, a fancier but something else, too. What else apart from pigeons does he talk to you about, all those hours you spend with him?"

"Ireland, ould Ireland, he calls it and. . . ."

"Yes?"

"Nothing else really."

"What does he have to say about Ireland?"

James licked his lips and scratched his head. "The orange and the green," he said at last, "he's got a poy-em about them, and he sometimes says it and he sometimes sings it and he has other songs too."

"He's a fanatic, James."

"What's that?"

"Someone who"—how to explain? He tried again—"someone who goes for an idea but goes too far, much too far. . . ."

"A martyr!" James exclaimed. Buzz was proud of him; it was a better try than his own. But James knew his *Fox's Book of Martyrs*, which he had taken in under Mr. O'Duff's tutelage and large slices of white bread and cold bacon as a double treat.

"Yes, one who could become a martyr but also . . . one who would kill others for this same, as we're calling it, idea: perhaps ideal is better."

James became even paler and more strained-looking. "But he would never kill Joshua for . . . he would never kill Josh, *never*. They're *friends!*"

Since Buzz was rosy of countenance, he never turned pale, but he sat back from the table and his cheerful face seemed to swell slightly. He said nothing because he so hated having to say anything at all and wondered what on earth one of these clever psychologists would make of the ghastly job he had to do. He could also hear the consultant's voice talking about the "childhood trauma." But then, the childhood trauma of losing Joshua had already occurred.

James was fingering his mouth, which he always did when he was nervous. "Has he killed Joshua?"

"I don't know, Jamie," he replied sadly, "I don't know. But we're desperate, and we have to think of everything, as everyone is always saying, every little thing, even impossible things. It is impossible that Joshua should . . . not be here in this kitchen now . . . but it's happened."

James got up and walked to the kitchen door; his hand on the latch, he looked back at his father. "I'm going to do the birds now. The squeakers are doing marvelously. I'm going to let them out so I may be some time, Father."

He opened the door and went out, shutting it behind him, but immediately reopened it and looked back into the kitchen. "And after that I'll go up to the house and help Mr. O'Duff with his pigeons."

"*God, no!*" Buzz shouted, jumping to his feet and starting forward as though to prevent James from going.

"Don't be silly," James said curtly, "he wouldn't kill two of us in one week!"

Unmolested, he was allowed to shut the door again and go to his loft.

Mr. O'Duff was in the yard, and there seemed no need for the visible jump he gave when James appeared. James was wearing shorts and sandals, the weather was suddenly hot and summerlike, he had made no sound approaching; Mr. O'Duff had the drinking troughs down from the loft; in dungarees, with rolled-up sleeves, he was scouring them to prevent coating with slime. He was bent double in the hot sun, in front of the yard tap.

But: "Bedad! You scared me for a moment," he joked. "I thought it was the po-lice come about a parking error of mine in town last week."

James had hurried up the drive, hurried in case he changed his mind. If anyone had reason to be scared, it was he, and his thin crust of confidence was for the moment threatened to find that Mr. O'Duff should express himself scared about a parking offense! James was not taken in.

"I'm not expecting you, Jimmy. Why are you not back at school?"

James glanced toward him with contempt, as if he could travel back to school just as though everything were normal, less than a week since he and Joshua had gone to school together. However, as it was important to appear to be on Mr. O'Duff's side, he said nothing.

"I like to know when you're coming, see."

"Why?"

Mr. O'Duff banged the side of the drinking trough with the hand brush. "*Why!*" he snarled.

A tremor ran through James, but he held his ground.

"You've always come regular times," Mr. O'Duff said more mildly. "I like things regular, the birds live regular; the birds and I live by rule. I know when to expect you and I know when not to expect you. . . ." He meandered on in this vein for some time till James asked if he could do that job for him, and red in the face, he straightened up and handed him the scouring brush. "All right then, since you're here do this job for me, there's a bhoy. And after you've done that, you can do your couple in the barrel!"

"I've done them," James said, getting down to work.

Mr. O'Duff clicked his tongue as though this were tiresome news. "Great guns! I never know where you are or when these days!"

James straightened up and looked directly at him for the first time. Mr. O'Duff was fumbling for the key of the house in the large pocket across the stomach of his dungarees. The boy had no specific idea of any kind, but his brain and powers of perception had been stimulated and alerted to the point when the smallest movement appeared to be significant. He thought instantly of the shed and the emergency key which he felt sure Mr. O'Duff had not intended them to know about. It was simply a careless moment that had exposed its existence, one of those less-than-alert occasions to which the most heedful adult is prone. And now, though he had known it all along, the fact that Mr. O'Duff locked his door every time he came out of

162

his house, even to do the smallest service to his birds, seemed extremely sinister.

Scrubbing, James said that his father did not think that Joshua had run away and waited for the answer.

There was none, and James looked up. Mr. O'Duff was lighting a cigarette, and he had never before noticed that his fingers shook as he did so. "Eh, what was that?"

James felt like saying, "You heard," but refrained from doing so. Instead he asked Mr. O'Duff if he thought Joshua could have been murdered. And Mr. O'Duff snapped back that he had already told James what he thought had happened to Joshua, and it was no use everybody getting themselves snarled up thinking about Joshua because he was going to be away a long time, and we, *we,* would just have to get used to it. Other folks had to.

He added: "Unless, of course, the police find him wandering. . . ."

It was all very convincing. Mr. O'Duff looked at the watch on his wrist and said that time was passing. When was James thinking of going back to school, then? And James answered not till Joshua turned up; he wasn't going back to school on his own and that was that.

Mr. O'Duff said he wondered if the brigadier knew that was what James had in mind, because he was a sensible chap and would be unlikely to agree.

There was an atmosphere between them now, a chill keenly felt by both, and Mr. O'Duff continued to hang around, and James made as long a job as he possibly could of the scouring.

Finally, Mr. O'Duff, evidently sensing this, said: "Hurry up, bhoy!" And then James prepared to carry the troughs back up the steps into the loft, and Mr. O'Duff said no need, they could be left in the hot sun for a few hours, it would do them good. He looked at his watch again and said: "Hurry off then, laddy, I'm off out!"

He had never spoken to James like that before, and as he was speaking, James was struck with an idea.

"Could I borrow your wire cutters?" he asked plaintively. They had borrowed certain tools, including the wire cutters, before and always carefully returned them, but today Mr. O'Duff was in no mood to play with kids, and yet on the other hand he did not wish to alienate his young friend, with whom he had never yet been cross.

"Go on then," he jerked his head, just slightly irritable, "and thanks for helping."

He was holding the key in the palm of the hand in which he held the cigarette, and now he went across the yard and opened the back door. He turned and raised a hand. "Be seeing you then, Jimmy. So long!"

Be seeing you, yes, but it was now understood at a time that coincided with the other time they came, after tea on a weekday. And at the weekend, in the morning before Mr. O'Duff's dinner, and not too soon on Sundays because he wouldn't be home from church. Sunday evening was permissible, too.

The tool shed was a gimcrack lean-to affair which had, properly, no right at all in the fine stable yard. It smacked strongly of a shanty Irish scheme of architecture. There was a tool rack of sorts and many earthenware plant pots unused and cobweb strewn, except for one small one under which the emergency key lived. James turned it over with his foot; the key was not there.

He snatched up the wire cutters which fanciers need constantly. Mr. O'Duff was watching him from the house door, half-inside and ready to close it as soon as he left, but as he emerged from the shed into the yard, James heard the telephone ringing in the house behind him, and Mr. O'Duff slammed the door shut and went to answer it.

Like one of the newly arrived swallows, James darted across the yard. The stable from which the steps to the loft rose had been converted into a double-double garage, with a pair of immense wooden doors on rollers at either side. The one to the loft stood open always, and the Mercedes and the motorcycle were parked side by side.

Long ago James had been shown how to open the Mercedes hood and had indeed done so when "helping" Mr. O'Duff to attend to the oil and water of his car. He first opened the driver's door of the car, and with the wire cutters in his hand he clipped away at any wire he could see under the dashboard. Letting the door fall to silently

164

without shutting, he opened the hood. He could not hold it high because it was too heavy for him, but he put in his hand and arm and peering inside he snipped away at every wire available.

The telephone in the house was on the windowsill of one of the kitchen windows which overlooked the yard; from where he would be standing to answer it Mr. O'Duff could see the back of the car, but the angle was such that he could not see the front. Neither could he see James slip away, well out of his line of vision, and emerge again farther along the yard, from the old tack room, the door of which was rusty and unused, and James feared for a moment he could not open it but succeeded in doing so after a hefty push.

"Sheer bloody-minded vandalism!" as the old colonel said (who once came to lunch). For weeks afterward Joshua and James had vied with one another in copying the tone of voice in which he said it. It had seemed to them extremely funny.

As he approached the cottage, running hard down the drive, Maggie heard him and came screaming around the fence at the motorcyclist angle, hair blowing out behind, her huge eyes now visible, like headlamps. She stopped upon the instant she saw it was James and, without loss of face, pretended she had only come out for a sniff around. She had got out through a hole in the other side of the fence at which, in her boss' absence abroad, she had been steadily working. Now, as James opened the gate, she lined herself up close to his heels so that her boss, were he to notice, would know that she had not been out so much as merely greeting James.

It cannot be said that James felt happy, but he had a distinct feeling of elation. His actions had been mindless and instinctive, sparked off, no doubt, by the wire cutters in his hand. His first instinct when he found he was holding them was to throw them far into the shrubbery, but his second was to put them in the pocket of his shorts.

The change in the brigadier was noticeable; he looked about ten years younger and sprightly; his movements were swifter and seemingly purposeful.

"I must go up to town early in the morning, even though it is the thirteenth."

"To tell Granny about Joshua?"

"That . . . and other things."

How thankful he felt that he had not yet paid in Sherbia's check; he would have done this in London because the local bank manager would have been startled at the sum, and Buzz would certainly have felt compelled to apologize for it . . . or so he thought. So he left the check where it was in his old trousers, forgot about it in fact.

The time had come for him to take James even farther into his confidence, up to a point, that is.

"James . . . come out to your pigeon loft a minute. . . ." It was important that Mrs. Flower should not overhear as she cooked the lunch.

The brigadier sat himself on a packing case, and James clipped away at the sharp ends of a new piece of chicken wire he had to put over a corner of the flight chamber. He had really needed the clippers. "About what I told you last night; it was only a guess, but it had the quality of inspiration, it really had. I felt I knew it, and I still do think that house is being used to store ammo of all kinds and sorts. But at the moment I am not going to the police."

"I was sure you would, Father. . . ."

"I would go at once if it were not that I think it may all have something to do with Josh's . . . I've been thinking all night, Jamie, and very often if you think all night you imagine all kinds of rubbishy fancies, but with daybreak I got up and Maggie and I went for a hike across the common and I can see that there really is some sense in what I'm thinking.

"Mainly it's that brother Cart. He comes and he goes, that's the first thing I ever heard about Cart . . . coming . . . going. It is simply not outside the bounds of possibility that he took Josh with him. Hero's tales, you know! He could have had Josh to himself all that afternoon and evening you and O'Duff were clock watching for the pigeon race. He could have made him drunk . . . or simply talked him into it. . . ."

"Into what?"

"Going away with him, mainly, to carry out all sorts of useful jobs of the kind a young boy can do. Running messages for one. He could be in Ireland having a whale of a time . . . there's always been this terrible streak of naughtiness in Josh, ever since he was tiny. He'll try anything once, anything, don't you remember, James, in Beirut?"

Yes, James did remember, all sorts of occasions when Joshua was the one to rush forward into any new experience at the instigation of anybody.

"But I must confirm, I *must* confirm"—he laughed a little—"what I know, or think I know. So I must see, or get you to see what is in those locked rooms up at the house. So what about it, old boy? You see, as I've just been saying, boys *are* useful quite often."

James was with him every inch of the way.

"So there's only one thing to do about it, and that is I must get into the house and see for myself. Since I am a fat man, it is not so easy. Since you are a thin boy, you can manage it better. So have a go."

"But the key's gone!" James complained unimaginatively. "I saw this morning because I kicked over the plant pot it was kept under, in the shed." He tactfully did not tell his father that he had been the first one to think of exploring the house. He had a feeling of wild impatience. "Why tomorrow?"

But the brigadier was thinking of something else. "Maybe, maybe I'm wrong, because if the contents are so important, why have a spare key in the shed?" He shook his head sadly, saying that there was a terribly amateur quality about the whole setup. "But fortunately, they *are* amateurs. And with amateurs you can use amateur methods of combat. Which is just what we will do."

James was thinking about the vandalism he had just perpetrated, but he was also remembering that Mr. O'Duff had said he had to go out, and at this moment he might well be struggling to start the Merc. James would go up to the house after lunch, but unofficially.

Mr. O'Duff brought out the bacon parcel and, opening it, stripped off a thick slice, and another, and put them both in the frying pan. He sliced two tomatoes and put them beside the bacon and some cold potato. Joshua had complained last night that he felt sick, he was having too much bacon, he said; well, he wouldn't be having so much more.

All night Mr. O'Duff had tried to get Cart on the telephone; he had a list of telephone numbers of the "stations of the cross"; he had the telephone numbers of several "camps" in Ireland; he had the telephone number of the rooms at which Cart lodged when in Liverpool, but though he had "been there yesterday," "was here last week," was "coming tomorrow," he could not pick him up and tell him the preposterous but positive news that, with a slight change of plans regarding the boy Joshua, an immense amount of money could come their way; cash from a Piccadilly bank, but the thing would have to be planned carefully.

He had to talk about it to his brother, and quickly. Cart would, of course, blow off his top to hear that Joshua had not been instantly disposed of, in the way Mrs. Furnish had been. He would be angry but not for long; he would be told that it was a blessing the boy still lived and that if Joshua had been disposed of by now there would be no chance of getting the cash whatever.

And oh, bhoy! The cash! The guns it would buy!

Mr. O'Duff overjoyed was a good deal more tiresome, indeed, unpleasant, than Mr. O'Duff his Celtic-twilit, pessimistic self.

He had been thinking hard and had found a new way out of the familiar problem of having to produce the kidnapped one before any money would be forthcoming; and then the involvement in the old police-trap thing.

The brigadier wanted his boy back, right? went Mr. O'Duff's thoughts.

He was prepared to hand over the money, etc. etc., to

168

anyone whose actions led to the restoring of the boy to him, right?

Right, Mr. O'Duff would tell the brigadier that Joshua was in Ireland and that he wanted to speak to him on the telephone.

Phooey?

Not at all at all. Joshua *would* be in Ireland and *would* speak to his father on the telephone. Behind Joshua would be standing either Cart or a third party, holding a gun which Joshua would be able to feel between his shoulder blades. He would have been told not to worry about being shot, which would only happen if he started anything and said one word more or less than he was told to say. He would tell his father that he had run away to Ireland with an IRA bloke he had picked up with *just for fun*. He was now sick of it and bored and wanted to come home; his companions were willing to let him go if his father produced X pounds in cash (the exact amount of the Sherbia check in fact). He would tell his father the absolute truth, which was that if he was questioned and gave answers about where he had been exactly and with whom these past four or so days, he would be assassinated. And Mr. O'Duff chuckled with delight, knowing how much the boys relished that word, "assassinated." Dear God! How clever can you get when you really snap out of it and try? It was the smell of money for the Cause, and within easy reach, that had created such an improvement, maybe only temporary, in the working of his brain.

But whatever it was, he turned it over, inside out and upside down, and he could not find a single flaw in the scheme.

It left him, personally, totally in the clear because Joshua would never, never tell where he picked up with this IRA fanatic who persuaded him to join them. It was a coincidence that Mr. O'Duff and his brother Cart, active members of the Irish Republican Army, on the admin side of course, should live so near to his home, and as everyone knows, coincidences happen every day.

The only thing that was worrying him now was getting in touch with Cart and trying to get him to come and remove Joshua as quickly as possible. Not that he was really nervous about the D day plans (the day after tomorrow), but it would make his mind easier if Joshua was got out of the way. He might, just might have to shoot Joshua in some emergency, and that would be such a pity now, since he was worth all that money to the Cause.

Mr. O'Duff carried the breakfast tray downstairs to the cellar carefully, as it would be another pity to fall and break his leg at this stage in the proceedings.

Joshua was lying on his back, knees up, hands behind his head, looking wilted. He was listening to the eight o'clock news and groaned slightly when he saw the contents of the tray, grumbling that it was *always the same.* He was getting sick of the same old thing at every meal, he said.

"Is that so, Lord Muck? Let me tell you there wasn't a soul in all Ireland not so long ago but thought themselves blessed that they received a small ration of bad potato every day of their lives and nothing else, and all because of the English bastards. You're spoiled!" he added as he left him in a huff.

Having put so many telephone calls into orbit, he left the kitchen window open slightly so that he could hear the telephone ring across the yard, and went up to the loft. Whatever happened, the pigeons had to be looked after; he lugged out the drinking troughs. He was shaking because he was not simply frightened of Cart, he was terrified.

He had disobeyed Cart's instructions but—and it was an important *but*—he was exchanging Cart's instructions regarding Joshua for glad tidings which would be of great benefit to, perhaps not quite all mankind, but Free Ireland in the event. If he could only get his news in before Cart got his anger out, it would be fine, and that was why it seemed a matter of life and death to get him on the telephone. It *would* happen that the telephone rang just as brother James was mucking about in the yard shed looking for wire cutters; he had the presence of mind to see the little spalpeen go . . . well not quite, actually, before he locked the house door and got himself to the telephone. Even if James had nipped up again into the loft for some reason or other, he could not possibly have overheard the conversation.

Still and all . . . it *had* annoyed him that James had been there at all.

And Cart, who had been at the other end of the telephone, the call coming from Liverpool, had been cool . . . cool. Mr. O'Duff's efforts to conceal the object of his call to anyone listening in were so ambiguous and confused that they took some comprehending. There was no great shout of understanding from Cart: "By God, Con, you've done well!" Far from it, he was cool . . . cool to cold, saying that it was impossible to discuss it on the telephone; he would come.

When?

Not sure . . . he would come, however, as soon as possible. All well otherwise?

It was disappointing, but he argued with himself reasonably that he could hardly expect more. In the meantime he must keep his captive in good health and condition, so after a pint of porter he got onto his motorcycle and sped into the village for a pound of sausages with which to vary his prisoner's diet.

19

But as they talked beside their loft, the brigadier and James heard the motorcycle coming down the drive; James rushed down the path, was just in time to see Mr. O'Duff going through the gates, and returned to his father nodding excitedly.

"One can shoot doors open, James," his father announced.

He went upstairs to get his gun, now hidden in a different place, and together they went up to the house, not up the drive but around the field way by the barrel dovecot, and followed by Maggie, close to her boss' heels. They had forgotten Maggie altogether, but then Buzz often did: Maggie, however, never forgot him.

"There isn't a door," James said, remembering; he knew the outside very well indeed; there was the big double front door, and there was the back door. At the far end of the house was an unfortunate Victorian outgrowth, as there so often is, but in this case jutting out behind, a billiards room; it also had shuttered windows, but it had a flat roof.

The brigadier stood looking at it; to climb up onto it would be possible, but hardly for a fat man. From there, drainpipe and sequence of slightly protruding corner-stones would, or perhaps better could, provide a sort of foothold which could bring the climber to the alternate stone vases of the balustrade along the edge of the roof, behind which crouched the windows of the top floor and maybe a door of sorts for roof inspection.

Staring so hard that he did not even look at James, Buzz said: "Now fetch me those old sneakers—know the ones? And very quick!"

Only then he noticed Maggie, mooching nearby, sniffing apparently absently but knowing exactly what was going on. He waited for James' return, pacing to and fro in the long uncut grass of what was once a lawn. He was back in less than ten minutes with the shoes.

"Now go away, James. Leave me to it, this is going to be very undignified, and I may look one hell of a fool in a few minutes, so take Maggie, dear boy, and go. . . ."

James said: "Famous last words," but obediently he picked up Maggie and went.

Buzz was glad James was not there to see; like many stout people, he was extremely light on his feet but he *felt* fat as he clawed at the drainpipe; he felt, too, a heady carelessness as though he had been drinking; he no longer cared whether he fell or not; he lost all sense of responsibility; he was the agile fourteen-year-old schoolboy again. He failed to remind himself that in all probability the pipe up which he was ascending had not been painted or attended to since before Hitler's war, but it was a sound Victorian job and erected to last a century at least. When it was within reach, he put his arms around the nearest column thankfully as a lover. He pulled himself up onto the capping stones and over into the warm lead guttering where he lay uncomfortably pressed for a minute, gasping.

Then it was only a matter of exploring the roof. He walked carefully, then turned the corner, and after a few steps he came to the leaded window through which Joshua had kicked his way, not so very long ago. He peered in, barely able to see, but after a few moments his eyes became more used to the dark; he saw that the window was situated at the end of a passage with doors on either side, three per side. He wasted no time in kicking away a few more lights and bending aside the old lead, making a much larger hole than his son had needed. He was soon standing in the passage, just where Joshua had stood, and staring with great excitement at the stapled and padlocked doors.

For what reason would anyone use such preposterous galvanized staple, hasp and padlock other than to guard something precious indeed.

He thought about James, waiting with Maggie in great anxiety at the gate of the lodge, perhaps. If Mr. O'Duff were to return suddenly on his motorcycle, having been into the village to buy a newspaper, perhaps James would detain him or even unseat him, and while he was thinking these thoughts he brought out his gun and fired carefully at the wood of the door, as near to the staple as he could possibly get without touching it. He fired five bullets and with each shot he was shaken with the shocking displacement of air so close to him. He put the gun carefully back in his pocket before attending to the staple; it was almost hanging off and needed a few wrenches to come off altogether. He pushed the door open . . . he did not know whether he cried aloud EUREKA or not, but the miracle was he had found what he had come to find. An excruciatingly neat pile of wooden cases containing, as he saw from the label which bore the name of a firm he happened to know of in East Europe, in all probability revolvers. There were some cardboard boxes, much lighter, containing holsters for them, and further boxes of bullets. They were in a neat squarish pile in the center of the room, an island of them, so there was plenty of room to walk around inspecting them. What astonished him was the amount. This was only a small attic chamber, but there were evidently six of them, and if the rest of the house was being used for similar purposes, which he was sure it was, there was a vast amount of ammunition stored, enough to keep a small war like the Six-Day War in Israel going to the end.

With his ears cocked for the sound of the returning motorcycle, he tore around the house. There were evidently four major rooms on the first floor, master bedrooms the house agent would call them, all similarly secured. And on the ground floor a large hall with an apparently large reception room on either side of the front door. He saw the green baize door to the servants' quarters, dived through and made a quick tour of the owner's living quarters. "Disgusting!"

He was handicapped by the necessity of hurrying. He reluctantly passed the top of the stairs down into the basement, having no time left for further exploration. He rushed back upstairs and, with more care now, made his way back to the ground by the same way he had ascended. He knew now exactly what he was going to do.

James was standing at the drive gate waiting for him, holding Maggie, who was shivering; she was a great shiverer. But James was shivering too. However urgent a matter might be, lunch had to happen, while Mrs. Flower looked not so much cross as offended.

"Sorry," Buzz said after he had eaten like a madman, dashed upstairs, changed into his London suit and returned carrying his dispatch case and umbrella.

"The thirteenth or not . . . I've got to go and I've got to get back quick!"

They followed him to where the pickup was parked, watched him climb in and start up. He remembered them suddenly. "Look after Maggie, James!" That might have been all, but he seemed to feel something more was required. Leaning out slightly, he cried passionately: "I've lost my wife and I've lost my son and I've lost my little nephew Fatty killed by a bomb . . . now I've damned well lost my head! I may not be home tonight . . . look after Maggie for me," he repeated.

He started off so suddenly that the tires appeared to

be throwing dust behind them like the hind legs of a dog.

James' head was lowered, and into the top of Maggie's honey-colored head he was muttering that it was Joshua who was the one to look after Maggie. "She doesn't much like me . . ." he was saying.

As his father disappeared, Mrs. Flower turned to James and observed solemnly: "Something big must be going to happen."

The pigeons had to be attended to, and the only thing to do about Maggie was to put her on the lead and tie her to a tree, giving her the exquisite pleasure of watching James exercise his young birds.

Maggie, in fact, today found this far from pleasurable; sometimes she seemed to withdraw completely behind her hair, which fell like a curtain over her face; behind it her eyes were so big that, compared in proportion to the size of human eyes, they were saucers so big that no space for face was left over beyond the long nose. If James had had time to lift aside the hair he would have seen her eyes at their biggest: Maggie knew all too certainly when a family crisis was in force. She sat stiffly upright, never relaxing for a moment, as James let out his squeakers, one by one, letting them have a quarter of an hour each, then whistling them in. And the whistling in was a longish process since they were as yet only in the process of learning instant obedience.

Then there were the couple in the barrel loft to be visited, and James spent a good hour with them. When walking back across the paddock with Maggie still on the lead, he wondered what had been happening up at the big house; no one had noticed Mr. O'Duff's return on his motorcycle; had he by now tried to start up his car, burst into angry shouts, as he often did, and telephoned the garage to come and help start it? At the barrel loft one was out of touch and now James could see plainly that the barrel loft served the splendid purpose of keeping him out of the way. He mooched back home with a feeling of extreme uneasiness.

That this feeling was shared by Mrs. Flower was clear;

she was standing at the little gate of the lodge, anxiously looking out for him. She was, in fact, doing some good old-fashioned hand wringing.

"Have you seen Mr. O'Duff pass?" James asked.

No, she had not but she had seen other things, from behind the sitting-room net curtains. There had been a whole team of police cars up at the house, they had driven up, and in a few minutes they had driven past on their way out. Mrs. Flower complained that she did not know what on earth was going on, but whatever it was she was not going to leave this place and go home till the brigadier was back home and that was that, so James would have to put up with it, she added, half-laughing, half-crying.

James handed Maggie over to her. "Look after her, Mrs. Flower, I must. . . ."

"You must what, James?" Mrs. Flower asked in a good attempt at being stern. "You'll stay right here by me."

"Mrs. Flower, I can't, I . . ." He wanted passionately to see if Mr. O'Duff had discovered the Merc had been sabotaged, as he called it in his mind; he longed to see the reaction, or even if it had been discovered. Yet on the other hand he was terrified that Mr. O'Duff might suspect James—but why should he?

James became reassuring, fatherly even. "Mrs. Flower, you and Maggie go and watch the telly, really there's nothing to worry about; you're getting yourself worked up, Mrs. Flower. . . ."

"Nothing to worry about!" she cried. "I could do with a gun myself, I can tell you."

James pushed past her and went into the sitting room, pulling up a chair and standing on it to feel for the revolver behind the books. It wasn't there, of course; his father had either found a new hiding place for it or taken it to town with him in the dispatch case. Mrs. Flower came into the sitting room as he was climbing down from the chair, and they stared challengingly at each other till James broke the spell by turning on the television.

"I have decided," Mrs. Flower said at last, "that I shall stay here, James, till I receive a telephone call; I feel sure that is what your father would wish. He won't let us down,

176

I know, and I won't let *him* down; if we don't hear, there will be a good reason for it and I shall stay and sleep here on that sofa. Someone has to hold the fort . . ." she added.

Buzz did, in fact, as he thought "get in touch" with Mrs. Flower; he sent a telegram asking her in the politest manner possible not to come tomorrow the fourteenth, he wished to use the kitchen for purposes of his own, he hoped to see her on the fifteenth. But he sent it to her home, and Mrs. Flower received it when everything was over, and the shouting too. It made her cry because how could he think she had gone home, that crucial day he dashed off so spectacularly with such frightening words as a farewell, leaving James and the little dog alone in the lodge? Men! Mrs. Flower sobbed, the cleverest of them could be so unclever!

He was back home at late afternoon and Mrs. Flower, faithful unto death, had left "something" on a covered plate in the oven for him. James did not hear the pickup stop, but Maggie did; she was alert and barking before the vehicle stopped outside the door. It was typical of him to make much of being a fat old gent struggling out of a car, for James' benefit and also as a background to one of his esoteric jokes which would annoy his sons so much. This time it was: "Enter Guy Fawkes," and he went around to the back of the pickup and pulled out his dispatch case, fatter than ever, and a new hideous dark-green shiny plastic suitcase. "I bought this for when we next go to Butlin's," he explained, determinedly jokey.

As it turned out, he was grateful for the food offered him by Mrs. Flower and ate it with seeming relish. But he spoiled her pleasure in his return by fixing her with one of those piercing looks which were so unnerving. "Didn't you get my telegram?"

No, she had not been home. He frowned, thinking what was to be done with Mrs. Flower. "I'll tell you what," he said cunningly, remembering things about women. His idea was that she should take the bus and go into the nearest town, have her hair done, perhaps, and look at the shopwindows, which he knew she enjoyed doing, and have an afternoon outing; there were things he had to do in the kitchen. . . .

Mrs. Flower was touched that he should take so much trouble not to hurt her feelings too much; she even accepted with a show of pleasure the five-pound note he carelessly handed her.

"And now," he said, "I had better go and change my kit. . . ."

Finally, when Mrs. Flower had gone on her outing and Maggie was put gently upon his eiderdown, there was still James, who was dealt with less kindly as his father firmly shut the kitchen door. "Bugger off!" was what he said.

But James knew when his father was serious beneath the banter; he recognized this mood and treated it with respect. He did what amounted to keeping a watch outside the lodge upon the drive. After an hour or two he had no doubt that "something was up." A police car came and went, and in the period of three hours, three vehicles, one truck and two vans went up the drive and shortly returned. There was a small van which stopped in the road outside the big gates, and James distinctly heard a broadcast voice and saw the driver speaking back into a microphone. Shortly afterward the van turned quickly, backing up into the drive, and was off.

The brigadier finally emerged from the kitchen about a quarter to seven with a tray of tea and biscuits, calling James in. They sat soberly facing each other in the sitting room and drinking their tea.

"Do you know what it is all about, son?"

"No, Father . . . is it something to do with Josh?"

"Indirectly maybe, but perhaps it's more . . . oh, I'm not sure what it is, James, except perhaps furious indignation that all this ammunition, meant to kill innocent people, is being so carefully and secretly stored here. Old boy, can you find out for me whether O'Duff is up there or not?"

"He's sure to be, he always is, I've never known him away for a night, or hardly ever. There's the pigeons; if he'd even been away for a day, he'd have asked us to feed

178

them and let them out. . . . Father, if you're going to blow up the place, let me get the pigeons out first."

"It's not an atom bomb I'm going to use, boy, the pigeons won't suffer, they're far enough away . . . make sure they're shut up. But even if O'Duff deserves assassination, I don't feel it's my job; he must be got out somehow, you help me think of a way."

"But, Father!" James was breathless with anxiety, he could not get out the words he wanted; after a struggle all he could achieve was: "Who are you against, I mean, if you don't want O'Duff blown up, too? I mean?"

"Anarchy, I'm against anarchy with its phony banner of Peace on Earth, that's what I'm against."

"Not a person, then?"

"Your O'Duff has been kind to you boys, very kind. . . . I don't care what the hell happens to him in the long run, but I don't necessarily want to blow him sky-high tonight, this May fourteen."

"Cart's birthday," James remembered with that clarity of memory found unexpectedly in the very young.

"Now, listen, James. . . ."

"But, Father, Cart's *birthday* . . . there's something about it, they are having a party, or something. . . ."

Buzz stopped trying to say what he wanted to say and thought over this latest bit of information, could "make neither head nor tail of it, boy," and brought a "very special kind of whistle" out of his pocket.

"Now listen, James . . . I've made twelve very homely bombs, not friction-sensitive; I bought twelve empty one-pound tins from the honey farm, packed them with TNT with the blasting cap inside, then the foot-long fuse goes into the blasting cap, light the fuse, and Bob is no longer your uncle. I knew what I was doing, but God, it made me sweat doing it!"

James shivered again in alarm, his face chalky.

"Don't worry, I have not put the fuses in yet; they probably won't go off on their own! But listen, *listen,* James, this is important, this whistle, I shall blow it and when you hear it, if you are still in the vicinity of the house, get away from it as fast as you bloody well know how, anywhere, but as far away as you can get." He paused for reflection. "But you won't be—I've a bloody good mind to lock you and Maggie up here somewhere while I get on with the job."

There were so many *buts* James could not get them all out; the main one was how would his father get in to "load up" the house. The answer to that was he would get in the way he got in yesterday, quite simply up the spout, and after dark . . . he did not add that this time he would be carrying a plastic suitcase with twelve pounds weight inside.

James nearly screamed: "But if you had an accident?"

"I've got to be careful not to . . . but of course it would be much nicer if I could walk in through the door with my case, as though I had come to sell a vacuum cleaner."

"Don't try to be funny, Father!" James screamed, with reason. It was his turn to tell his father to listen. "Listen *listen*, Father . . . Mr. O'Duff won't be out because, I . . . I've wrecked his car!" James was half-crying, gasping it out.

"Oh, well done! Well done, James!"

"He never goes anywhere major on his motorcycle, and I'm sure Cart is coming here, it's been mentioned off and on, coming here again soon . . . they might both be in the house."

"Now look, my brave James, let's cross our bridges when we come to them. Go and find out if they are there. You'll see the motorcycle and *two* cars if they are both there; if they are not I will shoot myself in by the back door. If they are in, when the bangs start they will get out quick enough or we'll have to see they do."

"But you said when the whistle blew I had to get as far away as possible. . . ."

"So I did, but when I said *we* would have to get the men out, I meant *I* would have to. No, go on, get on with it, James, an hour to sundown? Or more? Mrs. Flower, bless her, not back yet. She's keeping clear, I wonder what she thinks it is for? She'll have gone to see that old aunt of hers, shouldn't wonder. Come . . . let's forage for grub in the larder and you can beat it up to the house and come back and tell me what the form is. . . ."

But his brave James let himself go as he hurried up the drive; he sobbed openly; his frame of mind was that of a distracted nanny, left alone in the house with a child who has, without warning, become demented and started throwing the crockery about. Still, he had caught the sense of the occasion and instead of approaching the house directly he crept through the rhododendrons, reminded strongly of the time shortly after their arrival when he and Joshua had been childish enough to play cowboys and Indians in these same bushes.

It was getting late. Without actually thinking it, James sensed that the close of day had started; the thrushes were putting everything they had into their evensong. James observed the yard, the back door, the shed from afar and could see no sign of life, no fresh car and no, repeat no, motorcycle. He crept out of the shrubbery and through into the yard; avoiding the usual entry into the stable loft, he went through the harness-room door he had so recently reopened. The Mercedes sat sullen and silent.

He hurried up the wooden steps to find the loft exactly as it had been so long ago, yesterday morning in fact, with the drinking troughs reduced to one, the others still "drying" in the yard. He imagined rather than anything else that the flock had not had their evening meal and exercise, so he set to work at once to feed them and "put them to bed" exactly as he had been taught in this same loft by his kind friend, *yes, friend.* It took more than half an hour, and when he finally emerged, night was hurrying toward him; there was that added chill in the air which meant it was bedtime.

Pulling a bottle case up to the nearest kitchen window, James stood on it and peered inside, holding his hands on either side of his face to make sure he could see reasonably clearly. The kitchen was empty; he called, "Mr. O'Duff! Mr. O'Duff!"

He jumped down, relieved. He was definitely not there. In James' opinion the only thing that could have happened was that he had gone to the club in the town, which he often did, and he sometimes returned late.

He went into the garage and stood biting his knuckles

nervously; the lid of the hood of the Mercedes stood wide open. What was he to make of that, other than the obvious fact that the "sabotage" had been discovered?

The motorcycle had definitely gone. He looked around the yard for it; there was no doubt at all, it had gone. Mr. O'Duff had gone out on it to fetch help with the Merc? No, not that, not at that time of night!

James tore down the drive. "Father, Father!"

Buzz was there to meet him at the gate, Maggie wagging her tail and jumping up, welcoming the returned as she did if the returned had been out only three minutes.

"You can go now, Father, there is no one there, nobody. You can do it now. . . ."

"Keep calm, keep calm, Jamie boy. First let's shut Maggie into the sitting room. Now. . . ." The canisters being in the plastic carrier, the brigadier handed James the fuses, which he had wrapped in newspaper and put into a flat basket such as used to be supplied with fish. He tapped his old jacket pocket to make sure he had matches. They went up through the rhododendrons just in case someone should come up the drive. They went around the back of the stable block and through part of the derelict garden to the stackpipe against the billiards-room wall. They put down their burdens.

"Now go back home, James. I'll have to climb this twice." He pulled a reel of Scotch tape from his pocket. "I'm going to tape each one to the bottom of every padlocked door, twelve of them, and I mustn't forget the one in the cellar, which is the most important of all. . . ."

"Why?"

"Because an explosion does more harm starting from the bottom of a building than it does starting from the top. Now buzz off; I'll be half an hour at most, and if you hear the bangs or even only one bang, stay put; it doesn't mean I've been blown up, it means the op has gone without a hitch."

Reluctantly James went.

20

But now he was alone our brigadier looked askance at the stackpipe; anyone would have good reason to believe he had been drunk when he climbed it yesterday morning. He had a friend who had climbed Oxford's highest tower to perform that corny old act of putting a chamber pot thereon and who had later told him that he could never have done it if he hadn't been drunk; he had added: "Not blind drunk, mind!"

Perhaps whiskey was what he needed, and the thought that there might be a bottle of it in Mr. O'Duff's kitchen took him around to the stable yard again. James was a marvelous audience; how easy it had all seemed when talking to James: ". . . how nice it would be . . . as though I had come to sell a vacuum cleaner. . . ."

What was the point of that foolhardy climb up to the roof if it was not strictly necessary? And if Mr. O'Duff was really not at home, it was not necessary. He had learned how to shoot his way into a locked room many years ago, and he had been successful yesterday morning. He trotted off and brought his gaudy luggage around to the back door, placing them behind him and not upon the doorstep, as the vacuum salesman would have done. Four shots did in the lock sufficiently to aim a kick at the door, and it flew open.

After that, from somewhere a long way above himself, he watched himself as though at a movie, performing the sabotage act, securing the canisters on the floor against each door, taping the fuse upward so that it would burn down. He deliberately left the cellar to the last because that would be the last fuse he lighted, and in the event of the others starting to go off before he had finished, he did not want to be trapped by the cellar one going off on his way out. The trouble was he had no practical experience of this

183

kind of thing since his retirement and he did not altogether trust these fuses; he did not know how they were going to behave.

He had had to buy a whole box of tapers as they could not now be sold in ones and twos. A large packet of them, which had cost fifty pence, lay in the basket alongside the fuses; he pulled one out and tucked it down inside the V-neck of his pullover with a few inches sticking out. He patted his pocket once more to make certain he had the matches. He picked up the case and went through the open back door, along the passage, through the green baize door, past the top of the cellar steps and upstairs.

Somewhere, almost as though he were suffering from head noises, he could hear something unidentifiable. It was too late now, he had to go on up and hurry; even if it were Mr. O'Duff returned on his motorcycle, he would go on and get the top half blown off anyway. . . .

It had been his intention first to place all his canisters from top to bottom, then return to light the fuses, but the first three canisters were put in place so rapidly that he completed the top landing and left, rattling hurriedly down the top flight with all the fuses sizzling away as merrily as steaks at a barbecue.

The first floor, master bedrooms, was dealt with as rapidly, and he was laughing wildly when he descended to the reception rooms. Five minutes was what he had reckoned on with this length of fuse, but heaven knew what type of fuse they were since things ballistically changed yearly.

He soon knew. The first one went off on the top landing just as he was starting to descend the cellar steps. However, with the intention of being able to rush out unimpeded, he propped open the baize door with the now-empty case, and dashing down the passage, he opened wide the back door to the yard, hooking it back for safety, so that he could make the hastiest possible retreat.

But, horrors! in tore Maggie and started dancing with delight upon her back legs, steadfastly ignoring the fact that her boss did not show similar delight. That she had escaped from home and joined him was a matter for mutual rejoicing. The ecstasy of reunion was greater than any shock Maggie sustained from the really fearful bang that split the sky apart.

James must be not far behind. Buzz snatched at the whistle which was hanging around his neck and blew it hard; then carrying Maggie under his arm, he went down the cellar steps with the last two canisters and fuses. He put Maggie down and she went instantly to the door and started whining and scratching at it, making her excited whimpers and using her two front paws as though she were digging into a mole heap with all the soil flying out behind. Her paws moved so fast and so insistently that they were barely visible to the naked eye.

Inside Joshua, lying face down on his mattress, paralyzed with terror at the first explosion, recognized the sound, nobody could fail to, and screamed: "Maggie!" Just that faint cry reached Buzz's ears before the tremendous crash from the second canister. He recognized the cry instantly, of course.

"Stand back from the door, Joshua!" Buzz yelled. He had to wait the few seconds until the sound of the second explosion trailed away. "Lie flat!" He fired his revolver once and failed to perform the trick that had been so successful on the back door a few minutes ago. There were no more bullets in his gun, *or at home either.* He looked wildly around; there was no object whatever to which he could catch hold . . . he tore upstairs, followed of course by Maggie; excited as she was, frantic with delight at the prospect of being reunited with Joshua after all this time, her boss came first.

The woodshed! Thank God!

A sledgehammer with a broken handle and a very rusty pickax which dropped off the handle the moment he picked it up . . . but it was enough.

Shoved back onto the handle and wielded with the utmost care just once, at the first swing it hit through a bottom panel of the cellar door with a splintering sound which was totally blacked out by the third explosion from upstairs. The sledgehammer finished the slit and caused a hole, and with the second heave the whole panel fell splintering inward and out crawled Joshua.

He had to be dragged to the top of the stairs and out into the yard, and his father's next move was to attempt to return to put the eleventh and the twelfth and last canister in place, showing him to be the born soldier, the soldier before, long before, he was the father.

Joshua held onto his leg like a mad thing; he would not let him go, and Maggie, considerably shaken now by the terrible noise, thought it a game and tried to join in.

The soldier in him now running out like the bathwater, Buzz picked up his son and his dog and staggered out and down the drive, leaving the canisters with their fuses unlit, where they rested on the cellar's stone floor.

James came out from behind the stables.

"Come with me!" his father roared.

"But, Father. . . ."

"Come!" he roared.

After all this splendid bravery it is slightly shaming to relate that Joshua became intractably hysterical. That pound of sausages for which Mr. O'Duff had hurried on his motorcycle had remained unopened upon the kitchen table to be cooked instantly. Joshua had not eaten anything for twelve hours and had not been visited since his meal the day before at which he had complained about the lack of variety. Home and dry, he let go completely and lay upon the floor kicking and screaming, driving his father to the desperation of the remains of his liqueur brandy, a good quarter bottle of it, most of which he thrust down Joshua's throat.

There was no further sleep that night for anyone within ten miles; the conflagration made history. Within an hour of the explosions the house was burning with the ease of a gas-soaked faggot; the fire engines could do nothing.

Mrs. Flower, returning in a taxi from her outing and a visit to her old aunt, had the greatest difficulty in approaching the lodge, since fire engines from the surrounding districts were converging upon Mr. O'Duff's burning mansion.

As soon as she arrived and, gasping with delight, took over the care of Joshua and Maggie, Buzz and James went off to see about the pigeons. Already the fire had reached what Buzz had considered might be the optimum stretch, but the flames were reaching perilously far across the yard, even though it was by no means a windy night.

They found all the bird baskets they could, old and shabby as well as reasonably new ones, but even so they did not secure more than half the pigeons. Finally, as a precaution, they opened wide the trapdoors, and the remainder flew frenziedly away.

They would be back, Mr. O'Duff would say were he there, they would be back home, even if there was no home to come to.

The police threw a cordon around the estate, the firemen keeping watch to prevent anyone approaching. Fire engines thrashed through the rhododendrons, through the paddock, in across the old walled garden, through the wall itself, and yet their streams of water seemed totally inadequate.

"Oh, Father!" James kept gasping, half in tears, in terror and, somehow, in admiration.

Having done all they could, they retreated from the battle scene, down the drive; Maggie was leaning out of the bedroom window so far that it would seem her paws were strongly glued to the sill. She was straining to see in the red-tinged darkness. The noise was terrifying, but even above it they heard the earsplitting edge to her bark that she only used in a crisis.

And then, when the conflagration seemed to be dying down, came the tremendous bang when the fire reached the great heart of the matter. It was an eerie, finite, dome-shaped boom, and the blast caused a number of people to fall down or allow themselves to be blown down. It was talked about for weeks after, being described as louder than a lot of people had heard during the war; there were those who said they thought the end of the world had come, and someone named it the bang to end all bangs.

The excitement of seeing the blaze on television, the local television cameras having succeeded in being on the scene just before dawn, the frightful chaos and mess and, above all, the necessity of doing what they could about the pigeons kept the Patricotts busy for two days. The news brought pigeon fanciers, members of Mr. O'Duff's club, who offered to take care of the birds until the owner turned up, and James was kept busy putting down names and addresses and names and numbers of birds so that he could supply Mr. O'Duff with it when he returned.

But where was Mr. O'Duff?

The whole house had collapsed, the walls falling outward with that final gigantic blast; no one would say for certain if there had been anyone in the house . . . or not. The stable block still stood, but racked by fire the Merc was only just recognizable as a car and certainly not as a Mercedes.

It was only on the evening of the third day that the chief inspector came. Buzz sent the boys away. He was going to tell nothing until he knew how much the chief inspector knew and if he knew as much as the national newspapers, that was pretty well nothing that any other observer did not know; the house had evidently been used for storing explosives and weapons of guerrilla warfare, intended presumably for Ireland, and by some mishap or other had blown up, spontaneous combustion or careless storage, who was to know? "A man" was helping the police in their inquiries.

Buzz could barely believe that the man was not himself. With every hour that passed he expected it, and even when the chief inspector finally arrived, the expression on his face was not that of someone coming to question a man suspected of arson and a whole lot more.

"I'd like a word with you about your boys, Brigadier. How well did they know Mr. O'Duff? In fact, I want to know how much you all saw of him, what sort of terms were you on, and so on."

Buzz told him, he told him the exact truth: how the boys had seen O'Duff almost every day, how the man had seemed to like young people, how he had given them pigeons and taught them to look after them . . . the lot.

"Did he ever talk to them about his secret life?"

And so it went on, but nothing was said about the last few days, the imprisonment of Joshua and the talks Mr. O'Duff had had with him as he lay on that mattress in the cellar. They had all tacitly decided to keep quiet about it until and unless they were compelled by circumstances to tell it.

And finally Buzz asked the question: "But where is O'Duff?"

"It was bad, very bad. I've questioned all the men who were there and they didn't like it—he had a very nasty unsavory end. Well, this terrorist your boys met up there from time to time, it seemed he was a monk until he was over thirty, a holy man of fine education: Father Carthage. Terrorist, extremist, call him everything you will, he boasted that he had never killed a soul . . . there's ambiguity for you . . . it's a typical Irish characteristic, ambiguity, charming really, like the Irish are, unless they've gone sour. He carried a small revolver, and he used it to threaten, but he never fired it."

The brigadier expressed surprise.

"Except to kill his brother! As one of the Irish drivers we questioned remarked and I must echo: 'Isn't that enough to make the angels weep?' "

It took time but the chief inspector faithfully told him the lot. They had been after Cart O'Duff for quite some time, as one of the big boys importing guerrilla material and other arms into Ireland; once a year for the past five years, in the spring, there had been a big movement, all very skillfully organized.

This time they'd had the tipoff from one of the drivers, not himself an Irishman but a Pole. "Loyalty, that's the trouble in a big job like this, and Cart O'Duff must have known it. There's always somebody, when you're employing casual labor, whom you can't trust, no matter how much you're paying him, always *one* to blow it all up!"

Buzz stirred uneasily.

There had been a big turnout of police with a section instructed to go to every one of the prearranged places of call and the ports (Cart's unpleasantly named "stations of the cross") and about seven o'clock on the evening of the night actually planned for the big lifting operation, the ex-Father Carthage O'Duff was found in this wayside café called the Ring o' Bells, a mile or two from the M1. He was sitting at a table with his brother Mr. Con O'Duff who had driven from his home on his motorcycle to meet him there, and they were discussing something, some hitch, perhaps, in the proceedings.

Buzz knew what they were discussing; he felt in his trousers pocket and there it amazingly was, crumpled but whole . . . the check from Sherbia.

"Are you with me, Brigadier?" the chief inspector asked sharply.

"Very much so!"

At a signal the chief inspector's men, two of whom were in plainclothes disguise, stepped forward and caught hold of both Cart and his brother, at which signal the rest of the police poured in and the brothers were surrounded.

Cart struggled wildly, brought out a gun and waved it, and in much less time than it takes to say it, one of the policemen seized his arm and the gun went off full in the face of his brother Con. It did not kill his brother instantly, but to everyone's distress, because even policeman have their feelings, ex-Father Carthage went down on his knees beside his brother and started to give him extreme unction, in Latin, as he died.

This knocked the stuffing out of Cart altogether; he had nodded a listless agreement to everything that had been asked him, and all he seemed in fact to care about was that his brother's body should be taken for burial to the family grave in Lismore.

"And we're getting an extradition order to have Carthage O'Duff sent back home to Ireland, where *they'll* have to deal with him. . . . So I'll leave it to you, Brigadier, to tell your boys how they lost their old friend Con . . . more or less . . . as you please."

Buzz nodded. It was all he felt capable of.

"But I will say this," the chief inspector went on, "this was a businesslike affair, the whole amateur thing, the past operations were completely successful. And they had this excellent radio operator who was able to keep in touch with his whole gang of drivers and have them alerted to call off the operation. Otherwise we would have had this whole bang lot coming all night in a procession, to pick up their load of armaments, and what a haul we might have had! But thinking it over, it does strike me as more than a coincidence that the whole outfit should have been blown sky-high on the very night that the lift was planned; it was more than spontaneous combustion, and it might well have been the chap that gave us the tipoff if he isn't as astonished as the rest of us, or seems to be. However, it doesn't matter; good luck to him, I say, there are that many fewer things likely to hurt civilians."

And then, just as he was going, he remembered something. "Oh, by the way, Brigadier . . . the Furnish murder . . . it may be she knew something about what was going on here. Late that Friday evening, possibly only a few minutes before she was murdered, there was a telephone call from her to my house. She told my wife it was urgent, not a question of immediate danger, but she wanted to see me as early as possible in the morning, since I was out late that evening; she told my wife nothing else, she left it at that. But what I want you to know is that if you ever thought you were one of the suspects in that murder, ha-ha, I thought I'd just let you know . . . you never were . . . that murder could have been done only by a right-handed person. . . ."

They both laughed; with each it was a different quality of laughter. With the chief inspector it was pleasure in his own powers of observation, and in Buzz's laughter there was just plain relief.

And then next morning at breakfast a shaggy youth lolled carelessly up to the lodge carrying a childish rook rifle. In a previous era his father, the nearby farmer, would have come with him, probably dragging him by the ear. He came to confess that one morning "weeks ago" he had played truant from school and had gone out shooting "with

191

this" and had shot a pigeon which he saw flying around "just up your back garden."

The Patricotts found this embarrassing, and so did the youth, but the youth explained that they had all had such a nasty fright the other night in what his father had called "the bombardment," he had confessed his crime in front of the family; he didn't know why, he just had. And as a punishment they had made him come up here and tell all, and he was sorry. It was his moment of humility if he never had another in his life.

And when he had gone, this being a moment charged with emotion, if not necessarily the right moment, Buzz brought the worn-looking check out of his pocket and called for Mrs. Flower.

"Now," he said, "this is an awful lot of money given me by my friend Sherbia, the Arab gentleman whom you have all met. He was pleased with the small service I did for him, and as I would tip someone fifty pence, he gave me this vast sum which is going to make a big difference to our lives. First, we are going to get in the pickup, boys, and scour the country for a school which will have you both, and I mean a boarding school, probably a minor public school, which is the British name for a private school, don't ask me why. Secondly, I shall look for another house or cottage, and if it has a greenhouse, well and good, and if it has not, I shall build myself a fine heated one, and make my fortune, or not, as we shall see, growing and selling hothouse flowers."

James jumped about, denoting pleasure, but Joshua, who had to be different, said that probably no school would have him.

"And Mrs. Flower," the brigadier said, "must have a small car of her own out of this windfall or fortune, whichever you like to call it, so that she will be able to look after us still, even if we find a new house that is not as conveniently near to her as this one."

Mrs. Flower acknowledged this gracefully and hurried from the room to continue her vacuum cleaning, but also to have a good cry. There was something she would so much rather have had than money.